34

34

Tanith Lee

Writing as Esther Garber

IMMANION
PRESS
Stafford England

34 by Tanith Lee, © 2004, 2nd edition 2017

Cover Art and Design by Danielle Lainton
Interior layout by Storm Constantine
Illustrations on pages 6, 14, 66 and 133 adapted from vintage pictures in the public domain
Illustrations on pages 77, 78 and 134 by Storm Constantine

Set in Garamond

ISBN 978-1-907737-82-4

IP0132

Author Site:
Daughter of the Night: An Annotated Tanith Lee Bibliography: http://www.daughterofthenight.com/

An Immanion Press Edition
http://www.immanion–press.com
info@immanion–press.com

CONTENTS

THE GARBER STORIES OF TANITH LEE

Storm Constantine

Tanith Lee wrote three books, for which she described herself as 'channelling' other minds, other voices. The narrators of these books were not invented characters, as such, but discrete individuals who 'worked' with Tanith to give their creations to the world. These narrators were Esther Garber and Judas Garbah, a brother and sister of Jewish origin. As she says herself in her essay 'Meeting the Garbers', they are not *her*, they are *themselves*. She merely provided a medium through which they could communicate with reality – whatever that might be!

While Tanith herself was utterly aware of how this might sound to people who aren't intimately familiar with the unusual ways writers' muses can behave – and manifest – at times, she nonetheless described the process honestly, didn't shy away from being regarded as slightly mad – or 'bats' as she called it – or pretentious. She always told it like it was. Her stories came through untrammelled, and she allowed them to manifest themselves as they desired.

The books by the Garbers are *Fatal Women*, a collection of stories and novellas, first published by Egerton House in 2004, and then in a revised edition by Lethe Press in 2013. The Lethe Press edition includes an additional story, 'Femme Fatale', and an essay on the Garber books by Mavis Haut, a dear friend of Tanith's, who also wrote *The Hidden Library of Tanith Lee,* a fascinating examination and exploration of Tanith's work (2001).

Disturbed by Her Song was published by Lethe Press in 2010. This includes stories by both Esther and Judas. The Lethe Press titles are still in print and available.

Finally, there is the book you hold in your hands – *34*, Esther's only novel – or, more accurately, it should be described as an autobiography. This was originally published by Egerton House in 2004 and has long been out of print.

Steve Berman of Lethe Press has kindly allowed us to reprint Tanith's 'Meeting the Garbers' in this new edition of *34*, which we felt would be of interest to readers who haven't come across her 'Garber' collaborations before.

Both Esther and Judas are gay, and their works are renowned for their unflinching eroticism, as well as the often unrequited or unsatisfied desire that rumbles through many of the stories like congested magma, ready to explode.

34, particularly, reverberates with denied consummation, the terrible ache of longing. The man-woman, Julie D'ouest, who torments Esther, is both a torturer and a cruel tease. Like Esther, we never discover Julie's motives and desires. She is a phantom, an expressed ideal, a kind of succubus.

From what Tanith says herself in her 'Meeting the Garbers' essay, it's clear that more stories and novels might have emerged from these fascinating narrators. The mention of a second Esther novel, *Cleopatra at the Blue Hotel*, is especially heart-rending for fans of Tanith's work, because now that book will never be written. So, we must make the best of what Tanith was able to give us, through the Garbers, in her lifetime.

34 is a very strange story, and often unsettling. Hauntings come in many forms.

MEETING THE GARBERS

(Adapted from the author's introduction to 'Disturbed by Her Song', published by Lethe Press, 2010.)

I first met the Garbers in the 1990s; that is, I met Esther, and her brother, Judas. Anna didn't turn up, though she subsequently sent me a polite and kindly note. In fact, I've *never* met Anna, not yet, despite being given access to certain portions of her own work, and recently one of Judas's stories, which it seems she assembled from Judean fragments.

Esther's first communication with me involved the viewing of a headstone.

This was an arresting event. She refers to it in her novel, *34*, but allowed me to see the stone first. Just as the novel describes it, it was carved, and of very new-looking marble, set above a neatly finished grave. It bore only the number that became the book's title.

The complete novel was given to me shortly after. And not a great time after that, the first collection – *Fatal Women* – followed. Some separate stories by Judas arrived a few years after *Fatal*, and were not included in the initial Esther collection. (Judas doesn't seem to care about this. He always refers to himself as a 'writer' – but does he mean by trade – or inclination? Has he been published elsewhere? I sense some subterranean work, via a small press of long ago, in French, or even an Arabic language.)

Back in the '90s, the Garbers were rather striking. (They still are, I would say.) Judas especially was, and remains, a very handsome man, naturally slim and quite tall, by now, I would guess, in his sixties, as I am. But time frames – with definitely Esther – are hard to fix. Her (and Anna's) childhoods at least appear to have taken place in Egypt in the 1920s-1930s; but then Esther also proposes a young womanhood in England and

9

France, between the two World Wars. By the mid-90s she should therefore (yes?) have been approaching or inhabiting, at least, her seventieth year – or her *hundredth*. But she looked to me then of a youthful appearance – approximately fifty. A smart and well-dressed woman, neither old-fashioned nor let-me-be-of-the-Now, she shows her ethnicity – presumably mostly Jewish; this less in her (excellent) pale complexion, grey eyes and lush, wavy dark brown hair (not a hint of grey in *that*), than in a sort of antique-coin type arrangement of her profile. Semitic she is. Judas, too, of course. He is besides a seemingly wonderful equality of half Jew and half Arab, with the definite resultant beauty. His hair is mostly still black, his eyes, if anything, blacker than before.

Neither of these people is especially warm and forthcoming, however. They are cool, if sometimes observant and witty companions. Both are quite guarded also. Curious, it always seems to me, when their writing is so determinedly open and *frank*.

They have – they did from the inception – make very clear the different spelling of their surname. Esther, of course, is *Garber*, which is recognisably European Jewish. Judas meanwhile spells his version *Garbah*. I haven't been able to learn if this is based on some variant, presumably adopted by his butterfly mother, or an invention of his own.

I firmly believe that both of them are not merely compulsively truthful, in the way less of the Confessional than of certain writers/story-tellers, but conversely strategic liars. I'm well aware too that neither of them will object to my saying this. (Would I dare say it otherwise?) Lying also has its part in an authorial work-kit.

They do, perhaps inevitably, fascinate me. And whatever they care to reveal, demonstrate, *tell* me, I find enormously interesting.

There is Esther's London (UK) flat, for instance. A weird apartment in its way, with a huge main room divided by a single step into an upper and lower 'terrace,' and with much smaller rooms – kitchen, bathroom, workroom, bedroom – leading off a gallery above. It has long windows and green curtains, and a view outside of tall, summer-rich trees and greyish stone, one of those inner London streets you suddenly find around Harley Street, the British Museum, or otherwhere. Between the apartment door and the outer front door to the flat, is a 'storage' area, (what exactly is stored there?), that also has a small guest bedroom with bed and *en suite* lavatory and shower. Esther parks her brother out there on his very occasional visits. She has said he has repeatedly requested she acquire a cat, so that he can admire and stroke it, when in residence. But she hasn't done so, and Judas denies all this. There is always a little scratchiness from both of them, when referring to the other. Or to Anna, actually. It can be seen anyway quite plainly in the text.

As for Anna – as I say, I've never glimpsed her. She seems a well-organised, clever, possibly erudite woman, any hang-ups, (as evinced through Esther's *34*), either well under control or – maybe – non-existent. She respects her sister's and her half-brother's (Judas is only related to these women through their father) literary work, but has her own agenda. She is far more successfully secretive than either of them. And too Esther's implication (in her novel) that Anna is – how shall I say? – *less* than she seems – may be indicative. I wonder if I ever *will* be allowed, or even able, to meet her? I'm unsure, if given the chance, whether I'll be eager – or dismayed.

Having said which, obviously, I have never met any of these three in the flesh. In the flesh, so far as I can tell, they do not exist. At least not in any form or body I have ever physically encountered.

Nevertheless, to state they are simply three more of the thousands of characters I myself have written about, or through whose *minds* I have been made privy to their lives, seems not to express any sort of truth at all. Though I would proclaim this in reference to any character of whom I've written – they are all real to me, more real, *far* more real than so-called Reality – yet with the Garbers some other categorisation must be found. I haven't yet found one. And for this reason, their narratives, which I undeniably write (long-hand, as ever), then type, are styled – for the sake of veracity, *never* obscuration or gimmick:

TANITH LEE

Tanith Lee writing as Esther Garber/Judas Garbah.

That they are both gay is decidedly not the reason. I have written about Lesbian and male homosexual aspiration, love, lust and longing in several other places. Just as I've written about, and as, 'straight' women and men, gifted sorcerers, murderers, gods, demons and saints – and anything else I felt, at the time, given to encompass.

Nor do I think I *do* write about E and J because they and I share Jewish blood. (I'm a mix – half Russian Jew, a quarter English – with a tiny dash of French – a quarter County Clare Irish, and with a feasible whisker of Russian, and a drop of Black blood – unluckily the last two are probably untraceable.) But Esther and Judas, (and I assume Anna), are far more proper exponents of the Semitic races than I am. E and J at least have the correct looks – and as I said before, that glamour you can still see on ancient coins. And they are far more seasoned, steeped in other countries and customs, for example, those of France, Spain and Egypt.

They are not me. *They* – are *themselves.*

Evidently, in this perceivably split-personality tract, I am both distancing myself and irrevocably attaching myself to the Garbers. But then, as with most of my characters, and in this instance far more than with any other, they too have attached themselves to *me.* When they are there, (often they are absent), they are clearly delineated presences, just *outside* the mindscape. And unlike the others, too, they remain largely clandestine.

How much more work they will give me I have no idea. I've never sensed a forthcoming library, not even a full shelf. I know there should be one more Esther novel. I even know the title: *Cleopatra at the Blue Hotel.* This promises to reveal how Esther and Judas first met, as adults, by the Nile. While a second collection of Esther stories and novellas, which includes some pieces by Judas, plus the odd half-glimpse of Anna, already exists. Two of these tales, incidentally, Esther and I wrote together. Lee is truly bats, one might say. Or not. It seemed to me those particular tales have a combined perspective. Certain things I could essay through Esther that wouldn't otherwise have occurred to me, and (maybe?) vice versa.

To go back to the first introduction and meeting: despite not taking place corporeally, it did begin through a viewing of that pure white headstone. I dreamed of it, in the 1990s, complete with its number: 34. In many Dream Books, a clean, well-kept grave can be interpreted as a brand new start. I took it as such. And about three weeks after began to write the novel with that name. I had the first sentence, and I had the sense of Esther Garber. Nothing more was needed.

More even than with all the differing kinds of fiction I write, the Garbers have given me a significantly *unlike* territory. *In* this world, and out of it, anachronistic (deliberately), time-twisting, utterly self-indulgent – why not? Why write in chains? – and experimental. Varnished truth and gloves-off lies: the exquisite question that never has an answer; the answer that *is* the question.

Thank you, Madame et Monsieur.

Tanith Lee, 2009

CHAPTER ONE

Women Are Creatures of Night

After my mother died I went to Paris. The weather was bad, and all over the roaring deck of the boat, they were being sick. Vomiting terrified me, as sneezing did, on a lesser scale. Anything that causes such a total loss of control and helpless removal from the attack of the world.

I had no cabin, had not been able to afford one. I'd stolen what money I had from my father. In horror, when a sailor approached, I let him lead me to some area below. Here in the dark we swigged gin, and then he fucked me against the wall. In the momentum of the storm, not being very big, he kept sliding out of me. I tried to help him and finally he came. Then he was abusive and told me to get out. Above, thank God, the storm was less, and we were at last coming in to land.

France was grey as the sea. Grey as my eyes. We were all one, grey gaze, grey place, the grey depression of life. I remember Paris as grey, but different, shining, and the river, too soft to be compared to metal. No leaves on the trees, for it was still March. The Cathedral. And the tall grey hotel, in which I took a little whitish room lit by the grey sky.

My French wasn't very good, and all I could understand was that it was impossible for anyone to bring me a cup of coffee. It was also impossible for me to go down and receive a cup of coffee. So I drank water out of the tap over the cracked basin, in the tooth glass. The glass was cloudy and perhaps had never been washed. All those lips kissing mine now, with every sip. But the water tasted iron, *dry*.

The hotel had a steady throbbing, like a sound but tired heart. The heating pipes, maybe, caused this. Outside in the narrow street, under the thin bare trees, a few people passed, and a child with a governess-looking woman. The child called, *"Maman, Maman."* The woman took no notice, and must have been the mother after all.

I thought about my mother. She had died by falling all the way down a staircase in her bright flame-coloured dress. The staircase was of marble. It was in my father's house.

I hadn't seen any of this, but when I had been summoned back from my college, I did see my mother lying on pink satin in her coffin, heaped round with hothouse flowers. Anna was there crying quietly, and my father, also with eyes full of tears, and his black hair brushed back, and his nails manicured, and the gold ring on his marriage finger. My mother too wore her rings, and a necklace of pearls two feet long, and a white lace dress. I wondered how my father could be sure the undertaker wouldn't strip my mother of her dress and jewels before he closed the coffin lid. In the evening, we had dinner, and the servants crept and slunk round and round the table, carrying things to my father, as always. Everyone looked blank.

It was Anna who told me what happened, although she hadn't been there either. They had been going to the theatre, and my mother simply caught the heel of her shoe in the hem of the long red gown. She fell over and over without a cry. Both her ankles, and her neck, were broken. She was thirty-four.

Once I had been told, I dreamed of her headstone, which was of polished marble, like the staircase, and decorated with roses. On it was only the number, 34. Nothing else.

In reality, the tomb – it was a tomb – was much more elaborate, and of course had her name and my father's surname, and her dates of birth and death, not her age.

When the funeral was over, nothing changed. We sat about in the big rooms of my father's house, and the evil secretive servants brought us food and drink, in which probably they had spat, and the clocks ticked and the fires crackled. Sometimes my father would talk about my mother. He talked about her as if he had loved her, and she was a great loss to him. Anna listened patiently with troubled eyes. Our mother had married our father when she was just under sixteen, by means of a lie, and Anna had appeared seven months later. A year after Anna, there was I. That was seemingly enough. In later years they had separate rooms, my mother's full of ornaments and flowers, and her dressing-room full of dresses, shoes, furs, hats, jewels.

At eighteen, Anna looked older. She had assumed a responsibility, and, although I know she resented it, even hated it, felt she must not put it down.

I guessed at what we were now. A turn-of-the-century picture, of the grieving noble prince, with his two loyal maiden daughters, who would lay down their lives for him. Our fate now might be the cruelty of a step-mother, who would force us to sweep the hearths and wear rags. Or else we would tend our father as he passed into a handsome and upright old age. When he was ninety, there we would be, stooped, as he was not, Anna a virgin still, leaning to him carefully with the goblet of tea or the chosen book.

My mother's face seemed to have disappeared. She had left in my memory only a pair of dark eyes, and the rest of her form, fully clothed, and her dark hair with the wave in it.

I knew my father kept a certain amount of money locked in a box in his library. That night I picked the lock and took all that was there. It wasn't very much, not really, less than I was given by him to live on for a term at the art college. The dew was on the grass of the long front lawn, as I left the house at first light the next morning. It splashed wet and cold on my ankles, and the air had a smell of smoke.

The hotel in Paris smelled of damp and dust, of laundering, of another place.

At seven o'clock, once it had become almost truly dark, I went down. In the lobby, the man with dyed-red or false red hair, was smoking, and drinking a *fine*. The electricity flickered oddly. He remarked to me, in English, that a tram was passing along the avenue. He eyed me, doubtful, for I was quite well-dressed, and a foreigner, but also young, and with not much money, or why would I be here?

Outside there was the odour of cities. I walked up to the avenue, and a carriage with horses was going by. Another lumbering tram, with yellow windows, lurched past. And everywhere things had been lit, the windows, neons, streetlamps, stars.

Stepping into a small cafe, I ordered a glass of wine, and a bowl of soup that came with bread. There were some labourers at the tables, but also a couple of shabby young women, on their way to their single tenement flats, after a day of unpleasant honest work. There they would light their oil lamps, wash their stockings, check their accounts, and at last sink into a parched bed.

How dreadful Paris was after all, before the spring. Nothing seemed beautiful, passionate, even emotional. Her awful history of revolution and war submerged under her pavements, as if rivers of blood had sunk into them, straight down.

The soup was good and the bread stale.

I was hungry, for I'd had nothing since the night before. When I went out, I heard them whisper behind me. Looking back, they were all as stiff as lizards, their bright eyes fixed on me.

Naturally, I went down to the river, and stood looking at it, and the impression of an island with Notre Dame on its nest. The lights were now yellowish-bluish. I glanced up into the sky, where rainclouds were curdling. I had that feeling which comes to me, that nothing is real, and that, though I'm not real either, I am quite alone, the other human figures moving about only illusions. Therefore, they don't – can't – matter. Even my mother, falling, breaking, down the stair, was not true. She was a story told to me by my hallucination of a sister. Perhaps I had even invented my mother, and all of it. Perhaps my father's house had vanished from the world the moment I turned the corner of the street. And the country from which I had come, that too.

The name of the river, Seine, means Womb, or matrix. The city was birthed out of it. But the river moves on, and away, and the city is left there, grounded.

I walked back up the sloping street to my hotel. In a doorway, a woman and a man stood kissing, then he turned from her, put her by, in order to light a cigarette. The flame cut his face out of the darkness, but not hers.

In the lobby of the hotel, the dyed or wigged man poised at

his desk and held out my key, as if he had been expecting me all night, but I had been gone only a couple of hours. He said something in French, which I didn't grasp. Then he leant forward, and murmured, "Some difficulty, mademoiselle?"

"No," I said.

"When will your mother be arriving?" he asked. "Or – *vôtre père – peut-être...*"

"*Merci,*" I said. "*Bonsoir.*"

As I went up the stairs, I could hear him tapping his fingernail against his porcelain teeth.

In the room, I switched on the bedside lamp. It had a rosy shade that made the whiteness less bleak. But as I drew the curtains over the windows, they would not entirely meet, and through their thinness the street-lamps pierced like moons.

I sat on the bed and took out of my bag a sweet I had bought at a Turkish tobacconist's. Peeling the wrapper, I sucked the sweet slowly. It had the taste of honey and nougat and apricots. The room was cold, for they had switched the heating off, presumably for economy, or, conceivably, from malice. I thought I would go and take a bath in the rusting bathroom, and then come back and sleep. But I lingered over the sweet, which made me think, not of Paris, but of riding on a magic carpet above gemmed spires and orichalch domes. In fact, where should I go? Perhaps I could do better in the countryside, some farmhouse along a lane of poplars, with geese in the yard and badly-guarded girls. Or I could travel on, taking trains wildly across the continent, until all my father's stolen money was gone, or reduced to nothing in a score of *bureaux de change*. I might then end somewhere where no one could speak to me at all, nor I to them, we could not make each other out, and would be levelled to gestures of participation or fury. It would be like a sort of birth, coming again among utter strangers, speechless and knowing nothing.

There was a gentle knock on my door, the number of which was seven. I sat waiting. I knew who it was. Presently he spoke.

"M'mselle... Are you there?"

I was there. He knew I was.

About a minute later, he unlocked my door with his master key.

He stood smiling at me in the lamplight, which made his false red dye even more red. His eyes were reptilian and sad.

"What is it?" I asked, not trying to speak in French now. I assumed he was going to wheedle or threaten me for sex, but I would only uncross my legs and lie back, let him get on with it. I would not hinder, nor help, unless he requested it, as the sailor had.

"Now," he said, *"alors...* I suppose you might wish to make a little money."

"Oh, yes." That hadn't occurred to me at all, but it would be useful, obviously.

"Well, m'mselle. There is a – a young gentleman, who very much would wish to come to see you."

Again, I was surprised. But perhaps all the young women who stayed here were visited by young gentlemen. Perhaps I had missed the nature of the hotel. Once more, it could be useful.

"If you like. When?"

"Exactly now, m'mselle. If you will."

"Now?"

"Il attende – he is below. This very moment."

"All right. But please ask him to bring me up a bottle of mineral water."

The dyed man laughed. "So little? He will bring you wine."

"Oh good. But I'd like the water for the morning, please."

The dyed man lowered his eyes. He said, quite fondly, "You are just out of your school. Your black stockings and little pinafore." Evidently, he had a fantasy of English schoolgirls. I smiled politely and he went out, backwards, as if retreating from royalty.

Then I got up and glanced in the cracked glass above the cracked basin. Not from vanity, I didn't believe in myself, so how could I be vain. But I wanted to see what he had seen, what the other would *see,* assuming I could be seen any way. But then they would not see *me,* only the me I or they conjured up.

In the mirror, I was only pale, with long brown hair, which I had undone. A figure to be seen on a thousand young girls who have never done anything muscular and who eat only a little. But the eyes. The eyes are there. Look how they look back at me, so that my face vanishes, as my mother's has. Will anyone see these eyes? Not illogically, they may actually be the one item – or pair of items – that will not be seen at all.

When the door opened again, I was back, sitting on the bed, my chin on my hand and my elbow resting on the night-table. I meant to look relaxed, so he would not become anxious or aggressive. I'd had some experience of the violence of sexual encounters, even the gardener who first had me, telling me once that he had killed a girl for frustrating him. I had immediately answered that some people were wicked and were better off killed, and over his face had gone a look of relief, almost of discovery, as if he had found somewhere to rest a moment. He had raped me quite gently, pleased to be encouraged, not thrust away, and afterwards, when I said that I would always love him but I didn't expect his favours again, for I was too young – I was thirteen – and inexperienced to hold his affection, he kissed me, and said I was a good girl, and always to remember he had been my first lover, as he would always remember I had been a virgin.

But who came in at the hotel room door? It was initially not to be seen. A tall thin creature, black cloaked, and in a tall silk hat. Like my father setting out for the opera. A man of fashion – and wealth; face occluded.

I sat up straight, and gazed, and a gloved hand came out, holding a bottle of golden wine, which was already opened. And then the other gloved hand, holding two glasses by their stems. The glasses, though so negligently held, were of cut crystal. Not the utensils of the hotel, then, or certainly not the usual ones.

"How kind of you," I said. "But were you able to bring me the water, too?"

The magician's hand set down the glasses on the chest by the wall. And as he turned his back to do this, in a swirl of the bat-wing cloak, he said, as I had, in English, "It will come."

His voice was peculiar, husky, almost a whisper, no resonance to it, the voice of an invalid, or lunatic.

The door had been shut. I thought that perhaps now an older scenario was to be enacted, something from a quarter of a century ago, during which I should be mutilated or killed. But, not believing in anything, how could I grow afraid?

Now he turned again, and sitting down beside me, handed me one of the rich man's glasses, full to the brim with a wine that smelled of honey, as my sweet – hidden in the night-table drawer – had done. As this happened, he tipped back his head in a strange gesture, and the absurd top-hat fell off on to the floor.

How handsome he was, my visitor. How beautiful. The looks of him were as achingly sweet as the nougat. Black eyes with foliaged lashes. A slim pale mouth. A sharpened delicacy of nose and chin. High colour in the cheeks. His hair was black silk – like the hat – and grown down to his collar. He leaned forward and said, in the whisper-voice, "Your name?"

"Esther."

He smiled and said, in French, but I understood, "She who tempted a king."

But I understood too, for now the voice came out pitched and quiet and clear, and the face was so close, and I saw – he was a woman.

I drew back and turned my head and laughed.

"Oh," said the gentleman. "So you see."

"How interesting," I said.

"I hope so. Do you object?"

"To what?"

"You were prepared, I believe, to – *baiser*. But with me?"

"Why not?" I said. "It will be easier, won't it?"

"Not decidedly."

The he who was she guided the golden glass to my mouth, like a tender mother assisting her sick child to drink. And when I had had the wine, the glass was taken and my visitor put his – her – smooth cool mouth on mine.

This mouth was scented with peaches, or it was the wine. I made no resistance. The tongue in the mouth, which seemed indeed perfectly masculine, though possibly narrower than a man's, crept in on me. It ran along the edges of my teeth, along the hems of my gums, as if able to see where it went quite well. Yes, she has dressed her tongue with something, some drug, for it tingles, and now my mouth is tingling, and this sensation spreads, upwards into the architrave of my brain, and downwards, too. I found I had lain back, and now the black bat is covering me, and I can't see what goes on, between us, under this night-cloak of a melodrama villain. But her long fingers are unbuttoning the blouse, and sliding, slipping in. Such cool fingers. There is a smooth ring on one finger, and her nails are

short and manicured. "Two flowers that bloom," she says. And
they do bloom, they are opening and coming into life and fruit
against her palms

And now she runs her hands and arms against my naked ribs,
as if to crush me, snap my bones. She lifts her face from my face,
and looks at me, shows me her black eyes and the fire in her
cheeks, and then slinks down me like a snake.

Her mouth is in the place now where, as a child, I played. I
haven't done so for years, was disillusioned. This is – much
better.

Alone I could never reach the end of pleasure, which
instinctively I knew must come to some destination, some
pavilion, some *arrival.*

But now the black cloak has drifted up and covered me like
a tent or fallen curtain, and under it I hear her breathing, and
even the soft sound her tongue is making, on a point of delight
that is my flesh. And I hear myself, and how I am making a soft
noise also, like a machine that can't stop.

Somewhere up in the ceiling I hover, surprised, thinking
about all this. And somehow from above I see her ebb up my
body again, like a black ray. She takes my hand and puts it to her.
I feel her, through a thin layer of some fine material. "Do what
I'm doing."

So I do with my hand to her what, with her hand, she does
to me. And my own fingers slip by the garment and the rough
fur and into the velvet hole of her, and in the shadow under the
cloak she is tracing my breasts with her electric tongue, but all
the while she is gathering herself, like a swimmer, gathering
herself for a great leap off into the sea, or the air, launched into
flight.

Her voice comes now, high and cruel, a child's voice in a
game. She says, *"J'arrive."*

And she drops on me, light, heavy, so I can't breathe, and as
her body spasms, her fingers twitch, turn in me, and I too spin
over the edge into a fit of ecstasy and hear myself crying "Oh –
oh – oh…" as I roll about the ceiling, astonished.

"There," she says. And something in French. "Lie still. Here,
drink more wine."

I drink.

"I will tell you my name. Monsieur d' Ouest."

Ouest...West. Madame... Monsieur West.

"Don't go to sleep."

"I've been travelling all day," I said.

"You're so young," she says, as if she is as old as the city. "What is it – sixteen, eighteen – a little girl. How strong a heart it is."

Her hand, measuring my heart, is on my breast, which blossoms up hard again in its female erection, the nipple tighter than a bud, a bullet.

"I don't want to, again," I said.

"Be quiet. I give you no choice."

She does not. She is doing new things.

Her tongue, which is a serpent, as perhaps she – he – is, goes down into the orifice of my ear and touches my mind, and a huge shudder goes through me. Inside my sex I am as awake as neon. She moves me helplessly, gently, over on to my belly as I find, under the cloak, I am all naked, my clothes lying all around and under me, like stripped leaves. She lies solid on my back, and with the tips of her fingers begins to tickle, up and down, from my armpits to my hips. So, pinned, unable to move, I convulse, half in choking laughter, half in surges of arousal. And as she does this, like a vampire, she mouths my neck, which melts. And then one of her fearful fingers wriggles down and goes into my final orifice, the anus, and for a second I am closed, and then my own pelvis rises up to drag her deeper, and I feel the rim of her ring on the rim of the ring of me.

"What is it like?" she asks. "Tell me."

But I can hardly speak, and suddenly a hot dark orgasm, the sodomous blush of whose fire I feel all through me, makes me scream very loudly. As I scream, I have a vision of the red-haired man with porcelain teeth looking up towards this room, and leering. But she is coming again, against me, gasping, heaving, and a little of her scented spit, cool as the wine, runs down my neck. And what happens to her makes what is happening to me go on for much longer, so that it seems it can't stop, and, from the ceiling, I decide that it must. I stop it.

We are lying side by side on the narrow bed, both of us narrow enough to be able to do this. She's still swathed in her male clothes, that cloak, covered and hidden. Most of me has been pared to skin.

I turned my head and looked at her. Yes, she could pass for a very young man, about twenty. She was male, masculine, but not *manly*. She had shut her dark eyes and lay there, drawing in breath. I had an urge to touch her breast, but where would I find one?

"You want more?" she asked, not opening her eyes. "No."

"Why not."

"That was enough."

"There is never enough."

"I can't stand anymore," I said.

She said, "Much more. I could show you. But."

I sat up and drank the last of the wine in my glass.

She said something in French. I said I didn't grasp it. She said, "Do you dislike men?"

"Who? No."

"That's good."

"But you're not a – you're not," I said.

She smiled, also sat up, and swung her long legs in their trousers, now closed, over the bed. She must be in her thirties. The tiny lines around her eyes and mouth.

"*Combien?*" she said.

I said, "Whatever you think it was worth."

"Nothing. Everything. Blood, bone. My chateau."

I sat, thinking she had a chateau, but more likely only an apartment in the city. She must be the wife or mistress of some man, and she took on this disguise, and haunted the low hotels, going with young women vetted by the amiable, bribed *concièrges*. Easy, stupid young women, who needed money. What would she give me? It didn't seem to matter now.

Exhausted I lay down again, and startled myself, waking long after, in the night. She had gone, leaving me the wine, and a faint perfume on the bed, powder, fruit, tobacco, not truly male. I got up and drank some more of the dry water from the tap, and wedged the rickety chair under the door handle. Outside, on the street, the lamp moons burned cold and would not set.

Thirty-four – I woke again in the pure grey dawn, thinking she was that, the same age as my mother: d'Ouest, l'Oueste.

Later, I went to the bathroom and had a bath, and all over me I could smell her scent, like the scent of the fur of a cat that had been in an orchard on a winter morning.

When I came back, by my door stood a tray. There were two bottles of *Marnet* water, two hot brioches wrapped in a napkin, a portion of fresh white butter, a pot of coffee, sugar, and a jug of thin cream.

I ate quickly, like coming to land. Only afterwards did I find under my pillow, the bundles of pretty notes, a ridiculous amount, and one of her gloves, male, made for a boy, in pale suede; like Cinderella's glass shoe. The money had been stuffed into the glove. I sat on the bed in my petticoat. They had put on the heating, perhaps in my honour. She must have told them to treat me well.

Never before had I been paid, in any way – except by a mouthful of drink or, more importantly, my safety, danger averted – for sex. Never before had I reached that peak, the pavilion of apex, the *crise*. I lay down on my side and thought of what she had done to me, touching myself, and quickly the spears of Arrival went up through me, groin to brain. That was the third time. I noticed a smell in my nose now like smoke. This had happened when I came with her, before. Did something in my head catch fire and then go out?

Downstairs, there was a woman cleaning, with a red scarf tied round her hair. The red-haired man was nowhere to be seen. I tried to ask her where he was, but she only grunted and went on mopping the floor. Life had made her impatient with anything that did not force a response, and even with that, probably.

I stood on the space outside the door. Sunlight let down a rain of pigeons, grey underlit gold, with slate-blue heads. Their feet were an exquisite pink, and they were just like the pigeons in London. Did I only imagine I was here?

"*Bonjour*," said the red-haired man, coming up carrying cartons of cigarettes, his breath brown with coffee. He had heard me scream in orgasm beneath the weight of Monsieur West who was Madame. "A day to go about, m'mselle."

I took out a five franc note and put it into his hand.

"*Merci*," he said. He smiled and went past me. I caught his sleeve.

"Who is…?" I stopped myself. "That man last night," I said,

"*l'homme.*"

"*Ah, oui.*" He winked.

Ingratiatingly, I tilted my head, exposing my young, white throat, hollow, my best feature, not yet spoiled, but near the nape of my neck, a flower of bruise, grape-purple from her lips.

"I should like to know," I said, "will – he come back?"

The man looked at me. "*Non.*"

"I mean – can I expect...?"

"Not at all."

"Who is it?" I said.

He smirked, of course.

I said, "Do you know?"

He shrugged.

I said, "I was given a name, but, doubtless, a lie."

He spoke in French, and I thought he said that lies were often the best course. He added, in English, "You won't be troubled again." He was enjoying this, because obviously I had not been troubled, it had been heaven for me. I was in love, desperate, wanting more, money or sex or both. I wanted to keep *hold*, but even the guillotine, I think, its promise, wouldn't have got out of him where she had gone, Monsieur West, d'Ouest, l'Oueste. Idiotically I wondered, had she journeyed west? West across Paris? But I would never know.

Maybe, merely, she was now with her proper companion, of course a man, some banker or politician. She clad, *frou-frou*, in carnation satin and lace, bearing him his coffee or chocolate. Once every full moon, she left her luxurious bolt-hole, and preyed upon servant girls, and sluts, in the cleaner middens of the city.

Nearby, something was burning on a stove, behind one of the shuttered windows. As I smelled that smell, I grew hard and I grew soft. I ached with lust.

I walked up into the avenue, and found a place to send a telegram to Anna. I told her that I was well and had met some friends. I didn't mention the money stolen from our father, or the money left under my pillow. Anna too would be carrying a cup of hot liquid to our father. While in her tomb my mother lay on her back; decay had begun to devour her, and to scatter her crumbs on the carnation satin of her coffin.

In the Egyptian city where I lived in childhood, the colours were not grey but pale yellow and pink, sometimes a dusty, tawny brown. The sky was really brown too, although it is always said to be blue. And at sunset, it was red above its river. That is the Nile, of course. The Seine is the Womb, and the Nile 'The Mother of Men'.

We had a flat at number 12, rue Des Palmes. It occupied two levels. Below us lived my father's servants.

The upper rooms were large, with high elaborate ceilings, where fans continually revolved. Enormous windows looked across the city, some with stained glass in their tops, but there were thick shutters too, ready to be drawn closed against a *simoom*. I remember hot dark afternoons, wandering about the flat, while Anna, a good little girl, was practising the piano in the vast drawing-room. In the gloom of the closed shutters, it was still possible to see the dust which filtered in any way, gathering around everything like smoke. Above the loud sound of the traffic in the streets, the shouts, the bellowing of bullocks, and of Anna's stammering Chopin, it was easy to hear the grazing of the locust wind scratching at the walls. My mother lay on her bed, a cold cloth over her eyes, which the wind had made sore. She could not bear the *simoom*. She said that it was like someone running a bow across the highest note of a violin, raspingly, over and over.

The door to my father's study and office was locked when he was away, as he normally was. I didn't know what he did. Otherwise there were the two bedrooms, my sister's and my own, and the nurse's narrow little room between, and her closet, where she was expected to urinate and defecate, and wash her face, although she was allowed to use the tub in the children's smaller bathroom. The other bathroom was the province of my parents and led from their room, which had a balcony.

In the guest bedroom, I was able to undo the shutters, and so look down across the terrace below, where the cook had his kitchen. Sometimes I would watch him, sitting beyond, yellow in the dust, like an impressionist painting.

In our bathroom, Anna's and mine, I would lie in the bath. Perhaps I was seven years old. The water was greenish, and high above, miles above, the white ceiling with its cornice and shadow. There was a frieze round the tops of the walls, storks or ibis, white on darker white. On one occasion, going in, I found a scorpion had come up through the plug-hole, or from somewhere. Anna called our nurse, a timid, old young woman, about eighteen – Anna, at nine seemed much older. "Look. Father says you must get rid of it, please."

The nurse trembled. She went whiter than the tub.

"It's all right," said Anna. "Fetch Ahmed, then. He'll see to it."

And Ahmed came and squashed the scorpion with a spade, there on the tiles of the bathroom floor, while my mother slept under her cold cloth smelling of lavender. Anna had been shocked. She hadn't thought the scorpion would be killed, only ejected.

Further down, there was a garage in which, long ago, there had been a Bugatti. Now Ahmed and Kamil lived there. Sometimes Kamil would drive my mother shopping in a large hired car. She must have been about twenty-four or twenty-six. She drank gin in the evenings. Everyone pretended it was water.

Up the hill was a mansion with pillars. Over its wall burst lemon blossom, which we could smell in the flat. But at sunset my father brought important men home and they sat in his white-walled office, smoking strong cigarettes, before and after dinner, and this blue effluvia mingled with the lemon scent. These men, sometimes, wore hats like red upside-down flowerpots.

One of them took an interest in me. He stood between me and the corridor, so that I was against the wall, and he tickled me under the chin, like the game with buttercups. Instead of asking me if I liked butter, he said, "Pretty little English girl."

Then Anna appeared, very serious, and she said, "I'm sorry Esther has been bothering you, monsieur." And she led me away.

I had a rest in the early afternoon like an invalid, on my bed in the hotel in Paris. Someone had made the bed, badly. Drifting between sleep and awareness, I wondered if I might go back to the house in England, if I could find it, if it still was there, as it mightn't be. I hadn't meant to send the telegram, and I had, so, because I hadn't meant to go back, I might.

About three I sat up, opened the drawer, and looked at the money in the glove, and at the remains of the nougat sweet, which had become hard and dead. After that I rose and powdered my face and put up my hair. I went out.

Along the river, people were selling things, flowers or books, *things*. When I looked upwards, I saw a winding ascending street with Sacré Coeur at the end of it, the height of it, like an iced white cake. But farther along was Notre Dame, and there I went.

The windows were indigo and rose red, inside, and a priest stood at a lectern reading aloud. It must have been a service, there were lit candles for lost souls, and murmuring. The priest was saying *He will rise*. I understood, even in French, he was so clear and dramatic. It was Jesus Christ who was being spoken of. I realized that it must be Easter; there were green balsamic boughs everywhere, smelling curiously and wrongly like Christmas.

When I came out into the waning pearly day, a man walked instantly up to me and handed me a card.

Looking down, I saw, lucidly embossed, the name d'Ouest.

"You will accompany me. M'mselle?"

I hesitated, but everything was a backdrop, well-painted and appealing, like the roofs of the Egyptian city I had seen from the unused guest bedroom. The man was shorter than I, with a sly, wise face, little black eyes.

Stupidly, I stood and half turning, gazed back at the elaborate carving of the Cathedral door.

The man waited.

"Where must I go?"

"It is a house, m'mselle."

"Is it near?"

I could recall Anna saying this, anxiously, when we were children and adult friends of our parents had wanted, or pretended to want, to take us out. *Is it far? Is it near?* And they, meaning to excite her – or to be cruel – had said, Oh, far away. Across the city. In the desert, in the park, by the sea.

"Not so far, m'mselle."

"All right."

He nodded, and we went away together, away from the Cathedral. As we moved around behind the big body of it, it seemed to me like a sphinx, lying there over the river.

In a side street, he helped me into a black car, polished and shining, and drew a rug over my lap. He it was who drove us away.

I was thinking, wondering if he was in her pay, and had been bribed not to report any of this to her husband or master. Why did she want to see *me* again? Surely, her actions of the previous night were a commonplace, and a few others must have been as pleased as I had. Or was it that she found me special? At the idea of that my heart hammered. It was fright, I thought, not desire. Unfortunately, if she wanted me so badly as this, she might try to smother me, entrap me. I might become bored. It might be horrible.

But then again, how had she known where to find me? Had I been followed?

I said, to the man who drove the car, "Did you follow me, monsieur?"

He replied clearly, over the car's noises, "Not I. Someone."

I'd asked the man at the hotel about her. He must have reported it. It was my interest then which interested her. And maybe she didn't like my interest. Maybe she didn't want to consume and smother but simply to strangle – kill – me.

We chugged into a street packed with tall houses that grew up into pigeon-blue roofs with windows set in, the unmistakable skyline of Paris. Plane trees stood along the street. There were iron railings, through which, here and there, a bush had put out tentative buds.

Everything was very well cared for, in the deepening grey of the late afternoon.

The car stopped.

I looked through an ironwork gate, up through branches, to a black door. Did I have time to count all the house windows before he told me to get out? No...

The chauffeur handed me politely out of the car, and above, a frothy lace curtain shivered back into place. Who watched me? Was it she? Or – he?

Whose house was it besides? I should run away now. I walked up the path, and the door was whisked open by an imp of a girl, about ten or eleven, with a curling fog of sandy hair.

"Come in," she said, "come in."

Behind her, a pinkish dog yapped and bared its teeth, and scuttled off.

Was she a maid, this child? Was she a *child*? After all, if she were eleven, once I was only twenty-four, she would be eighteen – Anna's age, older than I was now...

She wore a navy-blue dress with a pinafore, black stockings – I thought of Monsieur Wig-and-Teeth at the hotel.

I entered. The hall was dark, with a large window totally obscured by a black fern. A red curtain hung over some entrance, the corridor extended, and a flight of stairs.

"Go up, go up," said the girl with London fog tonged into curls. She seemed sly, artful. Isn't everyone?

I went up the stairs and the dog ran out again, a strange dog like a furry pig, and again yapped at me. And the girl said, *"Taisse-toi, Henri."*

Over the stair was a wide hall, a lobby, with a window and another prehistoric plant, and doors everywhere, and a pair of double doors standing open, on a floor like glass, in which all things reflected. I saw a piano, armchairs, bookcase, a table resting upon the back of an ebony elephant, all floating on this lake. It reminded me of my father's house in England, and yet it smelled quite different. It smelled *feminine*. And what does that mean? There was a hint of tobacco, but mostly sweets, candies, and the sweet polishes with which furniture can be rubbed, also a rose smell from a vase of pink flowers... but more than that, the tense, dense aroma of healthy female flesh, perhaps not quite impeccably clean, wrapped close and sprinkled with an expensive cologne.

She was rising from a dark green chair, a thin woman in a black dress, fashionable but with a silly collar of costly lace, and a long string of immaculate pearls. She was extremely ugly, and over her ugly face was piled a conflagration of red hair. It was her red-haired body I could smell. Thick and slightly like a whiff of stale dinner – and yet so faint on *her*, as she came nearer to me, that it must only permeate from her constant proximity.

"I am Madame d'Ouest."

"Oh," I said. "Really?"

"Yes." She spoke an English which was high-pitched,

starched and clipped. Her big hands lay at her sides, and she met my eyes. She was not unnerved.

"You are surprised, of course," she said. "Did you expect Julie?" Only here did she lapse, with the name, into a French sound.

"Who is *Julie?*"

"She paid you a visit at your hotel."

I glanced down at the floor and saw my reflection, walking on water like Jesus Christ, who would rise.

"Oh, but that was a man."

"Ah, but no, you realise quite well, m'mselle, that it was a woman. My sister, Julie. My elder sister."

At that moment a maid, a true maid in black and cap, but gaunt and grim, came in past me, nearly silent as a shade, carrying a tray. The scent of sweets intensified.

"Would you take a cup of Indian tea, m'mselle?"

"Do you think that would be sensible?"

"Perfectly sensible. After all, when will you be sure to eat again?"

I thought of the money in the glove. Was I supposed to blurt this out? I said, "I can go a long time without eating."

"Yes, it's the English craze, to starve. For the figure. Well, we will forget all that for now."

She went across her floor of water and the ghoulish maid was laying out a white pot of tea and tiny white cups, a plate of cakes and other confectionary, a silver box of cigarettes, fruit in a bowl – oranges, peaches – a decanter and two twisted glasses, so shiny and their glass so intricately cut, they looked fractured.

She sat down in her chair and motioned me to sit in another. So I sat.

I did look, once, at the long windows. There had been lace curtaining on none I had seen, and was none here. Had I mistaken that outside? Or was it only, that in coming up her path, I had entered another parallel world, where her house only possessed velvet drapes. Was she pretty in the other former world? No, I didn't think so.

The table was close to her hands, which were manicured, but with long oval nails. She poured out the tea for me, asking if I preferred milk, cream, lemon, or fresh mint. I wondered if she would poison me, and suggested she give me exactly what she would have herself.

She laughed, Madame d'Ouest, a nasty whinnying noise. Her teeth were tremendously good and much too large.

"Now, now – if I were wishing to drug you or harm you, it would be already in the cup. Or on a knife or spoon – even the napkin. *Eh bien.*" Another tiny spasm of French, as if to prove she was. "I will give you mint and sugar. You'll like this."

"Will I?"

"Oh yes."

She handed me the tea, and the cup did not rattle on its saucer; neither of us was trembling. Then she pressed me to accept a cake. They were very luxurious, small oblongs and balls infused with syrups and jams, patterned with marzipan fruits. I asked for a peach instead. She whinnied.

"Very well. They are from the south. They came in on the train this morning."

"From your chateau, then?" I asked.

She smiled as if I had been clever and she was pleased with me. "A chateau? Did Julie tell you about a chateau? Ah, the poor creature. She lives in the past. Once. Once there was, when she was a child, a lovely house in the woods, a view of mountains, and some olive trees – too wonderful. I never saw the place, you understand. Before I was born my father blew out his brains – some financial crisis. I arrived in the city, in a horrid little room that overlooked a gas palace – that is, a place where gas was stored, but they had to make it look like a palace, Greek, you see, with pillars. Oh, the smell of it, that gas."

Did she now then saturate her air with sweets and meaty stinks to dispel that memory?

After this she began to eat. She ate like a beast, not messily but savagely, her huge teeth shearing through the terrified pastries and sponges and petit fours, and now and then she would swig off her tea, like sailor's rum, always renewing the cup. She had offered me nothing else, but then I went slowly. I did not trust the succulent peach or the fragrant mint.

I watched her. She didn't seem to object. Indeed, I had the distinct feeling she *meant* me to watch. Suddenly I heard a peculiar sound, like some sort of little mechanical thing pushed up the stairs. After a moment, the pinkish dog-pig called Henri rushed into the room. The instant his claws met the over-polished floor he skidded, swirled round and round with all the grace of a skater, until banging into the leg of the piano stool.

"*Henri – Henri – Ici! A Maman!*"

As he passed me, the dog gave me a vicious snarl, but that done, having shown me where I stood with him, he slid and scuttled to the tea table, and there paraded on his hind paws, while Madame inserted a whole cake into his pointed snout.

With that he fell flat, slobbering and grunting, creams and raspberry juices frothing from his mouth, as if he were in the worst stage of rabies. In the midst of this, he lifted his lips to show me once more his fangs.

Anna would never hear a word against any animal, and would doubtless have made excuses for this one. Had I been wearing boots, I thought I should have stepped on him and squashed him like a cockroach.

"Now," said Madame, putting down her plate and lifting the box of cigarettes, "you must tell me what you know of Julie."

She did not offer me a cigarette, nor the something of green she poured from the decanter, despite there being two glasses. Maybe I had only failed to earn these extras by my reticence earlier over the food.

"I don't know anything about her."

"But you know, don't you, that she dresses in male clothing, goes into dismal hotels, and there seduces young girls such as yourself."

"Do I know that?"

For the first time she frowned. She said tartly, "Well, it happened to you."

"Perhaps, only to me."

"Ah, don't be foolish, M'mselle. You're not alone in receiving her favours. Nor did she select you, or follow you, as I have had done. She has her arrangements, here and there, and so, since you were willing, got you."

"Then that's all I know," I said, "what you've told me."

"But I've only told you what you know yourself, or could conclude."

"I hadn't concluded anything."

"But you wished, did you not, to see her again."

I no longer blushed, if I ever had. But something twisted a little in me. I had wound a scarf about the bruise on my neck.

"She left a glove behind," I said.

"A glove? There's always something. Weren't you curious, at least?"

I shrugged.

She arched her back at that like a tiger, and Henri gave another of his growls, but she stuffed his maw with cake at once, as if it might betray something she had not. "Poof! These English gestures. What does it mean? *Là et là*"

"It was something that happened. Of no consequence."

"How am I to believe that? The filthy patron and all his monsters heard your sexual screams."

I was surprised to hear her say something so blatant.

I said, "Do you always credit what fools say?"

She shook her head and made a downward thrust with her hands. In one burned the brown cigarette she had not lit, yet must have done.

"You're enamoured, mademoiselle. You wish to see Julie again to practise with her this unnatural passion condemned by law and church alike."

I stood up, and Henri, his evil face appliqued with crumbs, ran roaring at me, snapping. I stepped quickly back, away, not wishing to be bitten.

"*Henri – en bas!*" she cried.

Henri flew aside but hesitating still, slavering red sugary saliva.

"Very well," said Madame d'Ouest. "Come with me now."

"No."

"You must, or I shall call my maid. She was a prison wardress once. She will like to hurt you."

"All right," I said, "whatever you say."

She conducted me out of the room, Henri skittering at her side like a crab, and up further stairs, and up. We were going to the attic rooms in the blue roof, and sure enough at last a door was opened, and inside was a long, unfurnished vault with a sloping ceiling.

"Go in there," she said.

I did so.

Then she slammed the door and locked it, and I heard her steps going away down the house.

There was nothing in the attic room at all, a bare floor, and some beams above. A narrow window had bars across it, and behind those the night too was coming, it was getting dark, as it had not seemed to be yet, in the house below. A perfect prison.

I had been locked up before. At my English school, when I was fourteen, because I was caught smoking. An insane woman I knew only as Miss Much, had locked me into a wooden toilet behind the larch trees. Here, I sat on the wooden seat for hours, and watched birds passing a hole in the door. Not knowing what to do, I hadn't tried to break down the door. Eventually I was sick into the lavatory. Soon after, Miss Much came, and let me out. She slapped first my face and then both my palms, but only with her hands. "You can go in for supper now," she said.

Later I told Anna, who wrote to our father. Nothing happened, then, but in our summer vacation, both of us were removed from the school. I was always a difficult pupil, slow at my 'work', and 'wayward'. I elicited the most violent responses from persons normally reckoned to be quiet and moderate, such as Miss Much, apparently, although I had seen her beat a girl across the hands with a ruler, until blood burst up like scarlet flowers.

In the attic, I wasn't sure what to expect. I sat down on the floor, with my back to the wall. I thought of things in the recent past, since I had started with Miss Much, and going back to a time before, recollected how one day in Egypt, I found my way up a secretive stair of the apartment block at 12, rue Des Palmes. At last, I emerged on to the roof, which was a wide one, and discovered I had entered another world.

Here, the sky actually looked blue, and feathered with clouds that had drifted from the river. There were huts, such as the cook's kitchen on the terrace below, and some large clay pots that had verdant bushes in them, and a big cistern full of muddy water that perhaps collected from the rain, though I don't remember, ever, any rain in the city, only sunsets, dawns, dry storms, and winds.

All about ran chickens, and ducks with emerald heads, brought straight from the marshes of tomb-paintings, and two white goats were chewing some sort of grass. Women sat

TANITH LEE

everywhere, Egyptian women with long brown arms and veiled heads, and beautiful teeth some of which, sometimes, were missing. They had not paused, none of them, goats, chickens, ducks, women, at my arrival.

If Paris is built of river and rain, the city in Egypt was built of sand, as, when a child, I believed the pyramids to have been. Perhaps they were. Bricks made of sand and straw, such as the Hebrews had to contend with. But there are stone pyramids. Or the pyramids are only mathematical, illusions, like the picture of Alexandria or Cairo sometimes even upside down in the air, when seen from the desert or the sea.

The women were dust women or women of clay, warm and smooth. I wandered among them, and one took me under her arm. She was making something, I don't recall what, a garment or a meal, but this she did with one hand. She stroked my hair and said something to the others, and they all laughed. I sat with her, and she fed me pieces of a sort of porridge, which I ate hungrily. I watched as she milked the goats. At sunset, the women rose, and responded to the strange eerie cry I had heard so often going over the city, I thought nothing of it. They were offering themselves to God, partaking of God. I stood there bewildered as they went away from me, their souls floating in the amber sky, their eyes glazed with peace, like the eyes of the dead.

After that, gently, they sent me back below.

Long after the attic window in Paris was black, I began to grasp I'd heard a clock chiming somewhere in the house, and now it had chimed ten o'clock.

I felt cold. Probably the heating of the house did not extend so far. It was obviously useless to call or shout, and from the barred window, only the vague suggestion of roofs had shown itself. Bats and vampires and mystic burglars prowl over the roofs of Paris in fiction, but doubtless no one would happen on me.

In the morning, the bitch would let me out, or not. I'd have to think of something else. Her wardress might come to feed me, and it might be feasible to gain on her by way of conversation. Sex and amenable talk are often the means to diffuse the harmfully mad or the merely cruel. I'd realised after, that Miss Much might have been my friend, if I had known, as the girl with the beaten hands had done, how to provide other pleasures. She

38

had boasted, that girl, presently, that her bottom was scarred as if with a red-hot gridiron, and that she was now the favourite. She said she lay in Miss Much's arms, sucking the woman's fingers, and Miss Much would weep and caress her, calling her Baby, and Kitty.

Maybe even the horrible red-head wanted something, or could be made to want something, and so – my escape.

I fell asleep.

When the clock struck three, I woke up again. My bladder was aching with fluid by now, and I considered how lucky had been the former imprisonment, in the larch lavatory. But then, I didn't know how long I would have to wait. I went into the corner and pissed on the attic floor.

About ten minutes later I began to smell the sexual odour of burning.

At first, I wondered if it had come from my urine, some residue of orgasm. But of course not.

I returned to the window. Out in the city, I could see no lights, no stars, and certainly nothing on fire.

In the house, then? Why not. Ah yes, now something drifted under the door. A soft mist. The smoke. Was I frightened? I didn't know. But I went directly to the door and banged on it peremptorily. At that second, I heard the peculiar mechanical noise of Henri, the dog-pig, scuttering up the stairs. And instinctively I drew back.

Henri snuffled with canine catarrh. And then he began to jump against the door – bang-bang – in this extremity, he meant to get in and sink his teeth, still sticky with jam, inside my flesh.

I must have been bemused, because I only stood there, breathing in the smoke and beginning to cough a little, and listening to the dog jumping against the woodwork. But there was a rattle now, and again, and then the sound of something iron falling.

Henri barked. Looking down, I saw through the smoke, the key of my prison nosed in under the door.

I knelt, took the key, and getting up again, put it in the lock. The door opened instantly.

Outside, the smoke drifted in vague gauzes up the stairs through the hollow of an utter dark. The dog seemed luminous, and perhaps was, for I saw him clearly.

"*Merci*," I said.

Henri gave a sneeze. Then he galloped down the stairs away from me, and I followed.

Everywhere was black and in silence. Did the bitch and her minions sleep? Should I wake them up? The house it seemed was on fire, for everywhere the smoke was going, thicker as I descended. And now I coughed, and I hurried, and suddenly I was in the hall where the window was and the plant and the front door. No light was anywhere, and I fumbled with the bolts and the chain, and called the dog by his silly human name, which had corrupted him. He had rescued me and I should save him. But he and no one came, or cried out. Once I had the door undone, I left it wide and ran out, down the front garden, and through the gate. On the pavement, I looked back. Nothing seemed wrong with the house at all.

Along the street, a lamp burned in the budded boughs of a plane tree, thin bitter green.

Quickly, I walked away.

You find your way through Paris by the river. And once I had got back to the river, it was simple for me to return to my hotel.

In the upper streets, in the sombre hours of morning, it was a deserted city of wolves, things which crept through the shadows. Only once did I pass beneath a lighted window, though once too I heard a gramophone playing a song I didn't know. But on the bank of the Seine, there were people, eating and drinking, arguing, laughing, night-people, lit by the lamps. A boat passed on the river, bright as a sunflower. Several times I was stopped. But I pulled free.

When I reached the hotel, naturally the door was shut. I hammered on it, on and on. At last a ghost came, a pale, pale boy, who stared at me and let me in. He gave me my key without a word.

After I had got into my room, and switched on the lamp, I sat down on the bed. I had that feeling I have often had, that to try to examine what has occurred is to try to conjure proper feelings – of alarm, fear, rage. Really, I felt nothing, cared nothing.

I lay down and went back to sleep.

The singing of birds woke me when the dawn came, and later some thumping and movement in the body of the hotel.

Having sat up, I knew what must be done, and did it. I opened the drawer of the night-table. Everything was gone. Everything. All the money and the glove, and my half-eaten sweet also. I glanced about, in the rain-lit morning. Two pairs of stockings, left to dry on the radiator, had vanished. My hair-brush was no longer on the stand before the mirror.

When I undid my bag, most items I had left there were still there. And in my purse remained a few notes, though not as many as there had been.

When I went down, about 7 a.m., Wig-and-Teeth was at his station.

"You stole my money," I said.

He shook his head, and began to speak in French, very courteously explaining that he did not understand me.

This went on for some while, and when I stopped, I noticed the cleaning woman with the red scarf craning around a door.

"I shall go to the police."

He said in English, "Yes, very good."

I went back upstairs, and in my room I put the plug into the basin and ran the tap. I left it running and went out. In the bathroom, I performed the same operation, but I had here to add some paper to the plug to keep it from leaking.

On a landing, the cleaner met me. She looked into my face.

"What?" I said

You go out?" she said.

"Yes, just for a moment."

She said to me, "The bar, the bar with the fishes. Agnes." The name was given in the French way, *An-yess.*

'What do you mean?"

"Agnes. The bar with fishes. Rue Sac."

Then she turned and went off, hunched over her familiar broom, on which, for all I knew, she might go flying.

I passed the man in the lobby, ignoring him, giving over only my key. At least, I would not pay him for my stay, and there would be a flood to clear up, unless they found it very swiftly.

I had left fire running up one house and water running down another, but such symbols were irrelevant. It came to me that perhaps the broom woman meant to help me, and that, thinking I was a prostitute, she had given me the name and location of a protective brothel.

As I was crossing the street, a carriage bore down on me, and only by running did I avoid the bounding horses. When I reached the avenue with the trams, particular men seemed to glare at me. As I walked along, one began to follow me, and although I slowed down to allow him to catch up, he wouldn't do it, and I considered that the ugly red-head, if she hadn't been burned alive, might have set more of her spies on me. Yet, anyone might be a spy. In the end, I turned to the man who seemed to follow me, walked up to him, and asked in French what he wanted. At this he blushed. He said, in heavily accented French, maybe that of a German, that I had reminded him of his daughter, who had died in a train accident. I inquired in English, not having the French for it, if this was a threat, and tears burst from his eyes. Before I could do anything or think anything, he rushed away into the crowd.

A tram came and I got on it, and sat down, not knowing where I was going now, where the tram would take me, or if I had paid enough fare, or would be thrown off with a typically Parisian scene.

So then, I was borne by the Tuileries, where children and fountains played in the gardens, and by a monument on some kind of pillar with a brazen globe on it, and through a long old street, winding and rolling, and the tram clanking and groaning, and on balconies were pots of red geraniums, although half the trees had not begun to blossom.

At last the tram ceased in a square. Everyone got off it, including the driver. No one spoke to me.

As I too left the tram, I thought, Now I shall find the rue Sac. I'll walk straight into it, and there the bar will be, with the procuress, Agnes-Anyes.

When I came through the square, there were narrow streets beyond, over which hung the pale grey masks of Parisian apartments. I passed a garden behind a wrought iron gate, not like the Maison d'Ouest. In this garden, there were only leafless trees.

I meandered from street to street, and was lost, and saw a bar called *Les Jouers*. But there were no fish, nothing, only massed men sitting outside with cognac and newspapers.

Then I entered another square, but this one small, with all the buildings crowded close, and there were cobbles and a fountain. Women shouted to each other from one window to another.

The area seemed old, and the women, scarcely visible, timeless. But then a cat ran by. It was a modern cat, of pointed ears and sleek short fur.

About a half a mile from the square, I came out into what I realized was the rue St Honoré. And soon I passed a dark door set on the street, with a plaque, and this told me it had been the door of the yard above which Robespierre had lived. Down this very concourse, where now there were shops, the tumbrils had rattled, going to the guillotine. And on this very door they had later written things in blood. It looked shabby now. Yet, there was a shadow. I hurried away, this way, that, and suddenly I had come back to the river.

I stopped by a woman selling oranges, and bought one. I asked, *"Ou est le rue Sac?"*

She told me. It was easy. I went there.

The fishes were not. In a great opaline tank, five lobsters cavorted, with purple horns. Probably diners chose them for a meal, but the lobsters did not know, were spared the knowledge of what would become of them as sometimes, if not always, human beings are. Now they fought, and then relapsed, beautiful, alien, and fearsome, among their weeds and stones. This, their little world.

In the bar, a couple of waiters lounged, with their long aprons almost to their ankles. Where the mirrors glittered, a girl stood between the green and gold bottles. She was curvaceous and blonde, with a whisper of rouge, and yet a look of the wild. She had risen at sunrise and washed her face in a pool, taken her dress from a hedge, and dusted her cheeks red by using the tail of a fox. She ran to the city, and entering it, half-closed her large dark eyes, to hide the rumours of her cave.

I requested absinthe, and this she gave me, with a carafe of water and three pieces of grey sugar on a cracked plate.

I asked then, in French, if she spoke English. She shook her head. But when I said, in English, "Do you know *Anyes?*" she replied, *"Oui."*

"It's you," I said.

"C'est moi."

I offered her a drink, and she smiled and said, in French, that she would have what I had, and put on the counter between us another glass of the strange liquid, the colour of the venom of a snake, and three identical pieces of sugar on a resembling cracked plate.

One of the waiters laughed. They leered at us, and away.

After this, we went on talking without real interruption, and for over an hour no customer encroached on the bar. Our conversation was in both languages. I spoke freely in English and she in French, and we seemed to understand each other perfectly. Perhaps this was telepathy, or only that she knew English better than she pretended, and I French better than I knew.

"Someone told me to come here. A woman who cleans at my hotel."

"Yes?"

"I don't see why."

"For help, perhaps."

"In what way? Do you think I need help?"

"Yes, if you met with her."

"With whom?"

Agnes lowered her eyes. Her lashes were uncoloured but very dark by nature.

I said, "Have you? Have you met *her?*"

"Some years ago," she said, or I thought she did.

"Do you mean," I said, "Julie?"

And Agnes blushed.

I drank most of my absinthe, and was changed. My brain became more clear and my body less. I said, "Well, I suppose you won't talk about it."

"Oh, yes. Of course I will." Agnes began to look up and down along the surface of the bar, as if little things ran about there between our glasses. Her memories, possibly.

She said she came from a village a few miles outside Paris, had travelled in a cart, and it had taken from six in the morning until almost noon. She was meant to stay with an aunt who had a small house near the meat market, but she couldn't find it. She was sitting on a bench with her bag, when a man came up to her. Agnes had been warned about men and she got to her feet at once and tried to hurry away, but the man said he knew someone who might give her work, just the sort of work she had come to Paris to seek, waiting, mending, cleaning – all she could do. Naively she went with him.

He took her to an hotel – not, from her description, the hotel where I had stayed. This was anyway about three years before; she had been fourteen. He had conducted her politely to a room, up the back stairs, and left her there, saying someone would come to talk to her, presumably to assess her qualifications for a job. Agnes, with a little laugh at her sillier younger self, told me she sat on a wooden chair, going over in her mind how she must remember to say that she had won a prize given by the nuns for neat stitchwork, and that she cleaned her grandmother's house every Thursday afternoon.

At last, the door opened, and in walked a tall, slim gentleman.

Agnes looked at me for a moment. She said, "It was, naturally, Julie."

She and I averted our eyes, and she blushed again, and although I never did, perhaps I did. Agnes half-turned, and reached, with her rounded arm, for the absinthe bottle. She brought it between us and refilled our glasses.

The two waiters had disappeared. Outside, the day condensed. I didn't know what time it was, there were no clocks. A shrill note of light cut through the windows and in the street, beyond the awning, people moved, or they were shadows, illusions.

"I truly thought she was a man," said Agnes. "I was fourteen. I knew nothing. I thought babies were made by swallowing a bee, or sneezing when a man was in the room. First of all, she sat on the bed, and asked me politely where I came from and what I hoped for in the city. I was very shy. It was a *man*, and so young, he looked about sixteen, but also rich and smart, and handsome, handsome in a lovely way – not pretty, not feminine – but in a refined way. What I'd thought a gentleman *would* be.

In the village, the men were big and covered with hair, and smelled. Then he said, the gentleman, come and sit beside him, and because he was young, I risked it. I sat down. And then, he started to pet me, and kiss my cheeks and smooth my hair. And by the time he put his hand on my breast, I was all melted, and I didn't know what it was, only that I was powerless. And only when he touched me there, I mean the one place I knew I shouldn't let him touch me – my grandmother had said, I must never let anyone put their hand on me, there, until my mother had had a talk to me. She said, If I had to touch myself, when I washed, or during my courses, then I must pray to the Virgin Mary while I did it – so when he did that, I said, 'oh no, monsieur, please don't'. Although of course, I wanted it more than anything.

"And then he said, 'don't worry. There won't be anything to confess.'

"So I said, 'but you mustn't put your hand there.'

"Then he smiled and said, 'Very well.'

"And then he put his mouth there instead. And obviously no one had ever said to me this mustn't be done. When I came, I simply kept coming and coming, and tears streamed down my face, and in the end I must have fainted. When I came to, he had stripped me naked and I didn't care. I'd been naked already, as naked as possible. Soul-naked, like you are before God. He was holding me in his arms, and he had most of his clothes on, and I still didn't know this wasn't a man. I didn't feel ill or weak as you do after fainting. I felt light and free. He fed me strawberries, and gave me sips of champagne – yes, there was a bottle standing on some ice. He said my heart was very strong, and now would I like to make what had happened to me happen to him. I was amazed. How could it be? He assured me just by looking at me, just by the fact of my existing in front of him as I now was, bare, I was almost making it happen to him already. Then he kissed me, the kiss that once my brother did to me, but that time I couldn't stop spitting. Now it was pleasant. It didn't excite me as the other things, but it was lovely, like floating. And when he put my hand between his legs, I was utterly startled. Oh – can you imagine – I started trying to find it, his thing! But this searching about must have been nice, and he was very ready, I mean, she was. And suddenly he arched over me, and I did see

46

what happened. And in that moment, as she was gasping and stretched up like that, I saw it was a woman. You see, I'd looked at a man's tool, I'd seen them. My brothers had shown me, and later I had come upon the blacksmith when he was piddling in the wood, and I ran away. I knew you couldn't be a man without it. And when she stretched, she made a sound, and it was a woman's sound. I was very frightened for a second. And then I realised, with my own sex, it wasn't a sin." Agnes laughed. "Of course, it's a worse sin than anything else. Or so they say, don't they?"

The absinthe in the bottle had gone down. Somewhere out on the pavement there was shouting, as if the shadows had had to be reminded to pretend they were real.

Agnes looked as though she had been in a storm, or a bed, flushed rosy, her eyes bright and dangerous, her hair fluffed out as if standing on end. My feelings were complex, but what had I expected? Here was one who, as I had, had been with this firebird of day and darkness, Julie d'Ouest, man-woman, demon.

"And did she leave you or... not?" I asked.

"Evidently. At dusk. But she'd exhausted me by then. She had opened me up, from my private place all the way to my throat. Even into my brain. There seemed to be nothing in me but stars and warmth and – space. She simply went away when I was asleep. And I slept mostly all of the night and all the next day and night. Twice a woman came in with a tray. I remember it so well. First there was coffee and cream and sugar and eggs and hot bread and grapes. And then later there was a whole roasted tiny chicken and rice and chocolate tart and a glass of wine. I was so confused. I thought she'd come back. I was waiting. Then, on the second day, I got up and found some money rolled up in a blue-grey silk she'd worn round her neck, a sort of cravat or scarf. That afternoon, a man came and told me to get out. He said my bill had been paid and they needed the room."

I thought that after all perhaps my bill also had been paid at the hotel, where they had stolen my money and property. Otherwise they would have kept more of a check on me.

"What did you do?"

"I went out, and found my way to my aunt's house."

"Did you keep the money?"

"No."

"Someone stole it."

Agnes said, almost proudly, "My aunt."

"Did you see her again?"

"Julie?" Agnes abruptly said something in French that I did not understand at all. And then she added, "She had a sister. An evil sister."

Just then, many of the shadows rolled in from the street, and there was noise and altercation. The waiters burst back out of the walls. Men were crowding the bar.

Agnes said, "Go and sit at a table." She handed me the bottle and the water and the sugar, on a tray.

"I haven't got much money."

"I'll fix it," she said.

I went and sat down in the sort of state that drink or bewilderment induce. I had consumed both. Besides, I wanted to watch her, Agnes, and from a distance it might be better. This one who had done what I had done, and with the same one. She was my age now. Seventeen.

A fat man led one of the waiters to the door. He wanted a purple-horned lobster from the opal tank.

"*Ah, non, monsieur,*" I heard the waiter say, sounding embarrassed. "There's some trouble with them, some malady. I can't let you have it until the inspector passes them."

"But you told me this last month."

"Yes. I regret it. They think there may be some germ in the tank. But we have some river fish, a true beauty, monsieur, and with a lemon and cream dressing the patron got from his grandmother's own recipe book. Have a cognac on the house, monsieur, or an *anise*. Something to spark the appetite. You've lost weight, monsieur."

"You think so?"

My table was in the corner, in a blue shade. My head swam a little and I pushed the alcohol away, and drank the water, with the sugar dissolved in it. The customers arrived and departed with great sounds. All were male. Some of them joked with Agnes at the bar, or even patted her, her hand, her bottom, when she came out to one of the tables. She smiled in a friendly way, and I knew, if and when she was propositioned, she would say, full of regret like the lobster waiter, "But I can't, monsieur. I'm faithful to my lover." And she would seem to be saying, How I'd like to go with you, such a man of the world, so experienced and fine. But you know, a woman should be faithful, as you would expect your own wife to be.

I doubted she had a lover, was that only my jealousy – she had met Julie. She must – ah, yes, stay faithful.

I wanted very much to hear what she had to say about Julie's sister, Madame d'Ouest. But I was tired, almost bored. Probably, Agnes would leave me alone now, also bored, and certainly tired.

Then through the smoke, I saw there were fewer customers, and these red and somnolent, sitting over their wine and cigarettes. Agnes came to me with another tray and set before me a tomato omelette and a plate of bread.

"There's no charge. It's what I have."

"You're very kind."

"Yes," she said, "I've almost always been kind. The filthy world hasn't knocked it out of me yet."

A man called, and she went quickly to him, as she must. He put his arm and hand round her slim waist and rubbed her gently, but on and on, as he spoke, telling her something, his red hirsute face lifted up to her blonde one.

I ate some of the omelette, which was good. She had put a glass of white wine beside it.

All at once, one of the men reached my table.

He spoke in French, and I shook my head.

"*Une Anglaise?*" he said.

"Yes."

"You like *aller avec moi?* I like the English girl." I said nothing, and he said, "I give you some stockings. And some francs."

I lowered my eyes and said, "Oh, monsieur. What would my lover say? I have to meet him in half an hour."

"Your lover? Some nothing. Have he need to know?"

I gazed at him lucidly. "I tell him everything."

He laughed. He said, "Ah, you love. You learn. And then, *petite,* you are too old." But he smiled as he left me.

Agnes said, "Come to, dear."

She thought I'd been asleep, as maybe I had. My cheek on my

hand. Her face was amused but almost tender, the way one thinks to see the face of a mother or elder sister, bending over the bed.

I anticipated she would sit down, but she motioned me to get up. She said, "I go to my room now. I must be back by seven o'clock."

As we went out, the waiters were clearing the last table, sniggering. In the tank, the lobsters idled like beautiful toy machines.

"What's wrong with them, those lobsters?"

"Nothing. We tell the customers that they're sick, and then we tell the patron that all the lobsters are eaten, and we must buy more. He never visits. We split the cash between us. Or, I get a little share."

"Doesn't anyone ever argue?"

"Once. A drunkard. Jacques said to him, if you want the thing, put your hand in and get it. If you die of poisoning, that's your look out. The idiot put his hand in the tank and a lobster bit him with its pincers and he ran off howling."

She laughed, so I did.

The sky was pale as egg-shell, yet the moments of the sun had not passed. We turned corner after corner, going by sweetshops with candies in green and white striped paper. A burning-red parrot sat in a cage, looking sidelong with eyes like black buttons rimmed with gold. It whistled, and Agnes whistled back.

Somehow, it seemed the city was becoming more colourful. I wondered if this was due to the presence of Agnes. She had taken off her black dress from the bar, and wore a flame costume with blue and white borders, and in her ears were silver coins. In one hand, she carried a basket with a round cheese and round red apples. It was all cheap, even the fruit, which was slightly bruised, and her clothing had a tiny darn here, and a speck of something there, and her shoes were scuffed, but she was bright, and like a painting, with her puff-ball hair.

In the end there was a yard, with doors crowded on to it, an outside stair, and then her own door, which gave straight into a sort of garret room, with its ceiling half glass, the kind of thing poor artists are supposed to live in. In the corner was a sink, and a cupboard, and a round copper bath oddly like a turtle. At the other end of the room was a bed with a gauze curtain hanging down over it. Between, the floor was scattered with rugs and toys, small sailor dolls, a stuffed lion, a painted top, and balls, and a dog on wheels. I thought uneasily there must be a child, but Agnes said at once, "I like to play. I like to be a baby. They tried to make me into a woman when I was seven, with all the chores, and the hidings. And my aunt was just the same. I was her maid, and I worked in three houses too, and I had to give her three-quarters of my wages. But not now. Now I do as I like." She put the basket on the table and stretched out her arms, exalting, as if she would touch the ceiling, from which was suspended a carousel of birds and suns and moons, that revolved in the disturbed air.

After that, with a pole, she opened the sky-light. The sky had grown blue over her roof. She took a large jug of clouded glass from the sink, where it had stood cooling in tepid water. She slipped the beaded net from the jug and poured out home-made lemonade.

We sat on the floor, pushed off our shoes, drank the lemonade. Pigeons cooed down at us. On her window sills were geraniums, too red to be compared to blood. And in a vase was a spray of white blossom that had not fully opened.

As we sat, she batted at the balls, and spun the top. She put the lion in her lap and patted the dog, and walked the sailors to and fro.

I said, "Are you happy?"

"Completely," she said.

"Why? How?"

"I don't know. I'm sure it wasn't meant."

"I'd like – will you tell me about Julie's sister?"

"I thought so. You've met up with her too."

"She had someone follow me," I said. "And I let him take me to her house."

"Was it wise?"

"No, I don't do wise things. I just – do things."

She smiled secretively. She said, "In the house you went up to a big room and she gave you cakes and fruit, and tea and liqueurs, and cigarettes. There was a funny dog that kept yapping and snarling. Just when you wonder if she wants to adopt you, she starts a sort of argument. Then she forces you upstairs, with the maid to help – and she says the maid has been in a prison and will do things to you, break your arm, twist your nose out of shape. They lock you in an attic. They leave you there."

She paused and I said, "Yes. Exactly. Almost exactly that."

"I cried," said Agnes. "I cried all night, I thought they would leave me there to starve. I've heard what happens when you starve. It's a terrible death. I'd been with my aunt some months before this happened, but I never got over Julie. They always say you'll be punished."

"How did you get out?"

"The dog let me out. It knocked the key out of the hole and nosed it in under the door."

I said, "And when you got out, the house was full of smoke…"

"Just so. And I ran down with the dog in my arms, and out into the street, but then he jumped away and ran back inside, and the door shut with a bang. I rushed down the street and tried to make someone go for a fire-engine. But no one would, and so I went back, and there wasn't a fire. There couldn't have been one."

"Someone just made the smoke," I said. "And the dog must be trained to do the trick with the key."

Agnes said, peeling an apple, "Do you know how many young girls this has happened to?"

"You and I," I said.

"Oh, it's happened so often, it's become a tale all over Paris. The wicked sister who abducts the lover of her sister – or brother, in most versions – sometimes they are two brothers – locks her in the attic and sets fire to the house. At which the girl is rescued by a little dog."

"No one would believe such a story."

"No one does."

She offered me half the apple, and looking at it, its white heart was curved like the hips, the belly and pelvis of a young woman. And it too had a fertile core. Was this the apple's mystery? The reason for its use in Eden?

It was dismal, wasn't it? This nasty adventure I had had in company with so many – how many – twenty – thirty…

"Afterwards," I said, "what did you do?"

"I went back to my aunt's house," said Agnes, "and killed her."

Into my mouth I put the apple, the sweet white flesh with its ruby skin of sin.

When I looked again at Agnes, she was looking straight at me. Her creamy throat was biteable as the fruit. She smiled still.

"You see," she said, "my aunt had been very cruel to me. They were the sort of cruelties people say are nothing, or, if they exist, are done for your own good. Like beating a child until it bleeds. But she didn't do that. She took my money and kept me short of food, and on Sunday, she would have wine with her luncheon after Mass, but I had water. She said I was lucky to have the water, it was city water, and pure, not like the water of the wells and streams in the village. Also, she told me often I was very plain. She told me no one would love me because I didn't know to behave. If I spilled anything she said I was a wastrel. If I had a sick headache she said I lied, made a fuss, and was lazy. She said I should have been left for the wolves when I was a baby – but she lived in the past. There weren't wolves any more, in our village."

"But there were," I said. "They sent you to her."

"You mean the people? No. Wolves are kind. They look after their own."

"So, you killed this bitch."

"Bitch...oh, *bitch*, *yes*, she was. She had a weak heart. She always told me to be careful not to make a noise. She said I upset her, I was so stupid, it *worried* her heart. Then she'd breathe very fast and I had to break a capsule under her nose. It smelled – like fire – *damp* fire, something smouldering."

Agnes said, when she went home after Julie's sister had imprisoned her, and the dog Henri had got her out, the burning smell in the house made her think of the aunt's capsule.

So she went into the aunt's bedroom early in the morning, naked, just as Julie had made her, and she got up and crouched on the aunt's body, on top of the thick bedclothes, like the terrible painting, *Cauchmar*. And when the aunt woke, Agnes told her that she, Agnes, had met a man who had fucked her all night, fucked her until her virginity was worn quite away, and this man had said what he would like most would be to rob an old woman and then carve her up, alive, and sell her carcass to the meat market. And Agnes had promised to let him in. At that moment, the door of the house was opened below, by a child on the street

Agnes had given the key to on her way back. She had told the child to wait until the clock in the market struck seven, which it had just done.

The aunt reared up in a spasm.

"Her face went the colour of a plum, and she died. She died under me, as I sat on her. It felt like the other thing."

"Orgasm."

"She didn't leave me anything. She left it all to the Church. And I went to work in a dress shop. I used to sew, and sometimes model the dresses. I went on from there."

"You could have left her," I said.

"I didn't want to. I wanted to kill her. She was a deadly woman. She was like a bad drain. She killed in her own way. She had to be cleaned out."

"Yes, I see that. Did you want to kill the sister of Julie?"

"No. Did you?"

"Why would I kill anyone?" I said. "They don't interest me."

"But Julie does." Agnes lowered her head. She put down, very carefully, her toys. "I can tell you where to find her."

My heart stopped. Like the heart of the deadly aunt, if her story was true. But maybe it was only a dream, the one unkind dream to leaven the bread of her kindness.

"Where, then?" I said, like a schoolgirl.

"Ah," she said. She drew up her knees, and looked at me.

"Anyway," I said, "how do you know?"

"Her sister told me. Oh, she let it out by mistake. It was a description of a place. An old house in a forest. But I knew of it. So... I can tell you. Trains go to the village there. It takes a day and a night."

"You – made the journey."

Agnes said something I couldn't understand. I said "What?" She repeated it. Had she said Yes, or No? Or had she said – that she had only gone there in her mind, her dreams, her spirit?

"The red-head said the chateau wasn't there. Or no longer Julie's. Never mind. If you don't want to tell me," I said. "I can't afford a train ticket."

"Yes. You could find a man. You go with men. You don't care. And you're so beautiful," said Agnes, "you'll easily find a man who's willing."

"Then tell me."

"Make me," she said.

I waited.

And she said, "I can't have Julie, but I can have you. You can't have Julie. But you can have me. And if we have each other, perhaps we can have her too. The little part of her that's left on our skin. Inside us. Under our nails. Under our tongues."

The gauze curtain over her bed was a reminiscence of the Egyptian city. She brushed it back and climbed onto her bed, as a child would. She had taken off her red costume and next her camisole and stockings, and her knickers, which were all pretty, and of poor quality.

I had to look at her properly then. Looking for myself. Were we alike? Not really. She was more plump than I was, shorter. Spun tinsel at her groin, and her nipples the shade of apricots. I merely stripped my clothes and let them fall on the rugs by her toys.

We lay down, and she turned on her side and began to caress me. She was very gentle. It was pleasant. I felt nothing, nothing bad, nothing good. I returned her stroking, and kissed her, but my mind was distant, not thinking of anything much. It was like the moments before sleep, something I have almost forgotten, now, the soft drifting, calm, without hurry, and the destination oblivion, or the other world of dreams.

She seemed not to think me unwilling.

I began to try to see her as Julie had. And I thought I should probably try to be Julie for her; wasn't this what she wanted?

So then, some stray fondling of mine caused her to giggle, and I remembered what Julie had done to me, and at the same moment, Agnes said urgently, "Tickle me!" Like a child again.

So I tickled her, her neck and under her breasts, down her vulnerable creamy sides, and in the fair silver down beneath her arms. She screamed and kicked with her little feet, so I took her feet and ran my nails lightly along the soles, and she cried out: "No! No!" But when I stopped she cried breathlessly: "Again! More!"

I tickled her feet, and behind her knees, and the inside of her thighs, and so came up to the silk spindrift of her loins. She spread her legs wide for me, like a contortionist, and I ran my hands up under her, taking her satiny round buttocks, and spreading them also. I stared into the crushed rose of her genitals. Julie had tongued us there. I put my face to her sex. She smelled of incense and sea – talc, the liquids of her vagina. Cautiously, as if she might be too hot, I put the tip of my tongue into the velvet cleft, as had been done to me. At once more paroxysms of laughter went over her. Here, too, she was ticklish.

I began to lick her, the smooth restless nub I found under her fur. She shrieked and writhed, giggling, groaning, and between the childish laughters, she now made animal sounds, and the edges of her fingers came sliding on to my shoulders, slipped away, fluttering, clasping.

She tasted of paleness, like an ice-cream that has no flavour. Yet she smelled of mint. Her wetness was like rain running down a leaf. My own rhythm absorbed me; I licked steadily, fascinated, like a dog lapping dew from the grass, and as I did so, I squeezed her buttocks open, closed, playing her like an instrument of music that let out these mounting sounds. For now she gasped and groaned also in rhythm, as if ascending a long staircase. *Ah,* and *ah,* another step towards the top, another.

But we were in the sea, and I was swimming, slowly but strongly, and every stroke of my legs took me forward through the pale green currents. Ahead of me, holding me up, was a figurehead of heavy white marble, which had fallen from a ship. I pushed it ahead of me, backwards. And so we moved together, on and on through the ocean.

For ever was this. It did not need to stop. But I felt her swell, as if she had a sail. And then she began to call in a high lost voice, as if her soul had come out of her like a gull. Over and over again she called, on one note, taking little sharp breaths between. And I felt her muscles running under my tongue, strong waves of ecstasy, and her juices spilled by me. Her scent was of mint and cream. She could not stop, she would die. I did not mind if she died – not that I didn't like her – *because* I did – if she died in my arms. And then I felt her go out like a star. The last ripple ran through her loins. I drew back and leaned over her, and saw her as Julie had, dead, drowned. Her lids were blue and her nostrils pink, as if she had been crying, and there were tears on her cheeks. Poor child, poor child.

I got off the bed and went to drink some of the last lemonade, for now my mouth was very dry.

When I glanced back, she had returned, and she was laughing, softly, sleepily.

"I knew you could," she said. "Come here, come here."

I went to her, and we drank the lemonade, and then kissed each other. I knew from what she had said kisses pleased but did not excite her.

"I'm a virgin," said Agnes. "Did you notice? Well, I am. I've had all this, and I'm still intact. I think it was like that for the Virgin Mary. Do you know the old paintings where the ray of light pierces the glass bottle, without breaking it? It's like that."

She sat up and held me. She was warm, her skin moist, smelling of spring countryside, ferns and asphodel. Or only her talcum powder.

"Do you love me?" she said.

"No."

"I know you don't."

"You're lovely," I said. What a man might say.

"Now you," she said.

I shrank from her. "It's all right."

"No, I want to make you."

"No, I'm too tired."

"You're afraid. Wait."

She got off the bed, and as she went over the room, suddenly she did a little twirling dance. I had seen little girls do just this. The sun from the open glass caught her. She was ivory and rose-petals. So pretty. Nothing in me stirred sexually, but if I could, I would have done her good.

She came back with a bottle of white brandy, uncorked it with her teeth, and gave it to me.

It was a spicy drink. She too had a mouthful.

"Think of it," she said, "think you are Julie."

She put me back and sat astride me, and then she lay down, her weight on my body, and her longest finger went into me, like a slender cool worm.

I thought I'd better make believe, as sometimes I'd had to do with men, not to disappoint, if this might cause angering offence. But then she began to speak in my ear, breathless again, calling me by name. She said she couldn't bear what I did to her, I must stop, she would come and she would die, and she began perfectly to simulate, it seemed, the sounds she had made before, and for a second I wondered if they had not been real, but then I had felt the orgasm go through her very flesh.

All at once her finger in me seemed to touch some hidden nerve. I could feel her breasts pressed into mine, and she was crying and gasping and I realised that she squeezed her thighs together to bring herself on again, and it was real. Then I opened in some long, agonising sweetnesses, a kind of pelvic yawn, all my womb and my belly, and torrents of exquisite nothingness flowed out of me, as if I had dissolved, as if I had given birth in delirium to a ball of divine fire.

"You see," she said afterwards. "How can you bear to leave me now?"

"I can't."

"What a liar."

I was afraid she might cry or, suddenly, that I might cry. An awful melancholy swept over me. But Agnes got up again and put a record on to her gramophone, which had been hidden in a corner. We drank the brandy and danced, naked, apart, only holding each other's hands, as children do, sometimes.

We went back to the bar of the lobsters together. By then she had changed me a little. I had on a pair of her stockings, with little flowers on them, and some of her rouge on my lips. She had struck a match and charred a stick, and shown me how to rub soot on the edges of my eyelids.

In the bar, she sat me at the table by the wall, and she went off to her counter, and soon the place had filled with men, and she slunk in among them, laughing at them, for she had known all the pleasure there is, and she was sealed tight as a child.

The one that came up to me was young. He had an olive complexion, and he made longer work of it than the other, earlier.

First, he bought me a glass of wine, and then, he asked if I liked gentlemen, and then, if I would go with him to his room. Then, he inquired what I would want, and I told him, as she had instructed me.

"*Ah, non!*" *he* chortled. "*Non!*"

I sat there.

At last he said, "*Alors...*"And then in English, "Yes, all right. Such a nice girl."

Outside, he took my arm roughly, nearly angrily, and I didn't look back, to see her golden-silver head bobbing in a sea of men. The deep-sea lobsters ticked and marched over their sand. She and they were safe, as safe as you can be, here.

He wanted me twice, and didn't make out we were lovers. He gave me the money, and, as I went out, a slim grey cat came flauntingly up to him from somewhere in the room, and he picked it up, smoothing it and kissing it. Women were for sex, and the cat was for love. He was, after all, very intelligent.

On the street, in the lamped dark, I walked towards the railway station, following as ever where I could, the traitorous black River Womb.

One of the times when they took us out, and forced Anna anxiously to say, "Is it far? Are we going far?" the expedition was to a shrine or a small temple that had been unearthed on the banks of the Nile.

We went in a big shiny car that belonged to the man, for they were a man and woman, fairly young, he a friend of our father's. He wore a loose white suit, and he was very brown. He smoked cheroots. She was dark, with a pointed face, and slumberous, slightly crossed eyes, always under a huge hat. She kept a flask in the car with alcohol in it, and kept offering it to Anna and me. Anna primly, nervously, refused, but I wanted to smell the drink, which was so acid it made me cough. I could never have thought I'd ever drink anything so foul. I don't know what business he was in, the business of making money, no doubt. Why did they want to take us anywhere, two little girls of four and five, in socks and sandals, with their hair clamped in bows? To appease or please my parents – to practise for parenthood – maybe they fantasised they would sell us to some Arab lord. There was something unreassuring about the couple. And Anna had once told me she thought the woman was a witch. But Anna thought our nurse was a witch. When she was three, Anna used to weep under the covers in her bed in fear of the witch-nurse, yet, stifling her sobs, in case the nurse were not a witch at all, and might be hurt by them. Perhaps the couple – the Golden Couple, they were called – took us out meaning to turn us into frogs. And they were distracted from their purpose.

We drove through the city, Mr Golden at the wheel, and Mrs Golden laughing beside him. Everything gave way for the car, as it did for our father's vehicle, when he had one. Bullocks shat on the street in fear of it, and in the dusty blades of the palms, small boys sat mocking it in envy.

When we reached the river, we had to get out and go on a boat. We sat under the awning of brown thatch, and were poled along the green-brown river under the brown sky supposed to be blue. Women were lifting jars from the water, and Mr Golden eyed them. But Mrs Golden fanned herself. She had black feathers in her hat.

Anna and I sat with our legs together, as we had been told we must, which was hard as our feet dangled clear of the deck. The sailors on the boat moved indolently, their beaked faces now and then turning to us, like the masks of birds of prey. But when they spoke to Mr Golden they grinned and bowed over his gold ring. Conceivably, they wanted a bite at it.

There was, as nearly always, a lot of dust, and at the site of the temple, more than ever, but white like smoke. Men were going about the site, suited Europeans, and Egyptian men scrambling in their rags and turbans, these shouting. Anna clutched the book she had wanted to bring, a picture book, which told the story of Isis and Osiris. The shrine or temple was, apparently, dedicated to Osiris.

What had properly been got out, lay behind a grove of date palms. There were uneven steps, and then a court with slabs of yellowed stone sticking up. Two pillars, with capitals a mile away in the sky, had all over them the picture writing of Ancient Egypt. And there was a pair of legs, seated legs, enormous legs, with sandaled feet each the size of the picnic hamper the Golden Couple had brought, and a kilt across the lap, and then nothing.

"Poor fellow," said Mr Golden. He gave his smeary laugh.

Mrs Golden said, "It should be taken seriously, this. One shouldn't, laugh. Oh no."

"What, you believe he can hear? He hasn't ears. Who is it? Is it Osiris?"

"They think so," said Mrs Golden.

"How do they know?"

Mrs Golden did not respond. She looked in carefully-arranged awe at the bodiless being, sitting before us.

Then one of the Egyptians came, to offer to conduct them around the site, and Mrs Golden said they wanted to meet the man who was in charge of the site, but she didn't recall his name, or she had remembered it wrongly, because the Egyptian said they was no one here by that name.

The Golden Couple gestured elaborately. Were they embarrassed?

We went round the site. There was nothing to it, actually. Although to an Egyptologist, everything, perhaps. Anna looked at everything that was pointed out. Hers was not designed awe, like that of the Golden woman in her hat of bird-killed feathers. Anna was trying to be polite to everyone, as usual. The Goldens, the guide, the temple – Osiris.

I stole away behind the disembodied legs, and down a defile, where scaffolding and planks held things up or back. Men worked there, and no one paid me attention. There was a tank in the ground, a cistern, and from it grew a single plant, not a lily or lotus, something harsh and blackly green. Behind the tank, among some stones, against a wall of rock that maybe in fact was also part of the temple, I saw two blue snakes mating on a boulder. I didn't know what they did, but it seemed like a dance. One covered the other, and they coiled their bodies, like ropes, pulling some unseen thing towards some unknown goal. It went on and on.

Mr Golden found me here, and when he saw the snakes he covered his eyes and turned away with a curse.

Mrs Golden came hurrying up. "What is it? What is it?"

He grimaced, and pointed at the snakes, not looking. "You know what they say. If you see the snakes dance – that is, if you see them *couple*…"

"Hush," she rasped. "The child."

"Well, *she's* seen. No luck for her."

"This superstition. Now," she said.

"Do you want me to be impotent?"

"*Hush*, the *child*."

He burst out laughing, drew forth a cheroot, lit it. The smoke rose in the heat.

The snakes continued at their dance. I hadn't understood what was said, only that this was significant. I felt sorrow pour into me, like a foretaste of death. I thought my mother would die and my father abandon us. I saw myself and Anna in some vast wilderness, some desert, lost and alone. And Anna would try so hard to be brave. But I – I would run into the sun.

Anna appeared then, and she put her arm about me as if she'd heard me calling across the temple. She said to the Golden Couple, "That man wants some money."

"Bloody Arabs," said Mr Golden. He went away and his wife followed after in her clothes of black and white.

"Look," I said.

"Oh," said Anna, "aren't they lovely."

She saw only their beauty, the beauty of the snakes, not what they did, or what it might mean. But it meant nothing, surely, to us.

After the picnic, which we had in another grove, during which the Golden Couple drank champagne that popped and spilled and was, they said, warm, Anna and I were quiet. It was always expected of us, not to make a noise. If ever we did so, we were chastised, although by words alone.

The Golden Couple grew sleepy, or lustful. They lay back, cuddling each other, in the green, hiding shade of the palms. Anna read to me from her book, the story of Osiris. Reading always helped her. Always does help her.

Osiris was the most perfect of the gods and he married Isis, the most perfect of the goddesses. They loved each other utterly, couldn't help it, seeing in each other the mirror of their own perfection. But they had a brother, Set, a red-haired god who hunted. He was jealous of Osiris, tricked him, and shut him in a mummy-case of carved and painted wood. This was then thrown into the river and borne out to sea. It came to land again far off and a tree grew up around it, a magnificent cedar. One day, the king of that country saw the tree and had it chopped down to make the central pillar of his royal palace. No one knew there was a god trapped inside it.

"But meanwhile," read Anna seriously, "Isis was grief-stricken. She cut off all her blue-black hair and dressed herself in a gown of mourning. She hastened out across the world, searching for her beloved husband."

From the corner of my eye I could see that Mr Golden had put his hand into the top of Mrs Golden's dress. He was smiling lazily, and she lay still, as if asleep.

Isis came to the city of Byblos, and learned that a wonderful cedar tree had been taken as the house-tree of the palace, and it gave off such a glorious perfume that all the city was scented by it. Isis, who had already become aware of this heavenly smell, knew at once that it emanated from her husband, Osiris, and that he and his coffin must be trapped inside the tree. She therefore made friends with the maids of the queen, anointing them with another perfume, that of her own body, which was as powerful and marvellous as the aroma of Osiris, but different. The queen of course, astonished by the new scent, had Isis brought, and at once fell under her spell.

"Every night, while the queen slept," read Anna, "Isis would nurse the queen's child on sacred dew from her fingertips, and then laid him in a brazier of flame, to burn away his mortal part."

At this, we looked at each other. We didn't understand. Fire was dangerous and we must never have anything to do with it.

Anna went on, "Then, in the form of a swallow, Isis flew about the pillar that contained Osiris, lamenting."

"The child," said Mrs Golden sleepily.

I glanced headlong. But Mr Golden now had his back to us. He leant over his wife.

"Look how nice it is," he said. "Look how it loves you."

"No, no," said Mrs Golden. She sounded resigned.

Anna seemed vaguely frightened. She whispered, "Let's go over there."

We got up and went further into the palm trees.

When the queen came in and saw her child lying on the blazing coals, she screamed. At that, Isis revealed herself. She explained that she had done what she could for the queen's son; he would now be a great man. But she wanted the house-tree cloven and the coffin taken out and given to her. She was a goddess, so they did what she asked.

Then she returned to Egypt and, concealing Osiris's body in the tall reeds of the marshes, set about devising a magical spell to restore him. But before she could complete it, however, Set came by, hunting, under a red moon, and finding the body of his old rival, cut and portioned it into fourteen parts, the head and brain, the arms and hands, legs and feet, torso, intestines and heart.

Anna hesitated. She said, "How horrible."

I said, "But that's thirteen, not fourteen. Thirteen pieces."

We counted them over. Thirteen. "It says fourteen." We puzzled at this difference between the three and four. But then she went staunchly on reading how Set distributed the body parts in various cities by the Nile, where Isis had to follow afterwards, with her sister, finding each bit one by one. Then she put them all together, all but one piece, which had been eaten by a crab.

At this point, Mr Golden made a hoarse noise. We peered back, but they were hidden by the lines of the trees. We heard Mrs Golden spit rapidly several times, like a snake. Perhaps she *was* a witch. But then, so was Isis.

Anna read sadly that, although Isis was able to restore her beloved husband, even so, since he had already died, he must go away to rule the Lands of the Dead, in the west, beyond the sunset.

"Which piece of him was missing?" I asked. "Was it a hand, or a foot? Or a whole leg?"

"It doesn't say. Perhaps his heart. If he had to live without Isis."

Mrs Golden was calling us briskly, and when we returned into the grove, she asked if we had had a nice afternoon, and even wanted to see Anna's book.

She was sour, but smugly practical, as if she had carried out successfully a chore she did not like. Her husband lounged under the tree, and had produced the alcohol flask.

The piece of Osiris, the fourteenth piece, was his penis. And it was the unmentionable item that the crab had devoured. Isis made him another by her magic. In some versions, this penis is inverted – a vagina. Even so, she conceived from it a male child, Horus, the hawk.

When we went back to the boat, and passed again the excavated temple, Anna looked at the statue, sitting with its feet on the ground and nothing above the hips. She said, with the profundity of childhood. "Perhaps Set took the rest."

There is another memory which adheres to this one, although it's much more brief, and must have been much later, when I was about ten, and Anna eleven.

There was another boat. A very large one, and some sort of official dinner had been held on it. Anna and I, in stiff white clothes, sat to one side. We felt very ugly. The evening before, we had somehow angered our father, who had told us we were ugly, naughty little beasts; he was ashamed of us. Here and there lurked other staid children, drilled to 'good' behaviour, scared to make a noise, and bored half to death. But the adults, who had access to hard drink, were having a fine time. They were noisy, too, and there was even a little orchestra.

Beyond the openings or windows or struts, I can't recall what they were, the glasses of the sky were honey-red, and the river was molten pink with draining sunfall. Servants were lighting more lamps, and the band was striking up, and we saw our mother dancing.

She was only twenty-seven, I suppose. How young that seems to me now. My mother, who died when I was seventeen and she was thirty-four. I am so much older at last than my mother.

She had on a copper dress with copper beads, and a red-embroidered panel at the bosom, and rose-red shoes. She was the belle of the ball. And those feet, so light, that would finally betray her on the marble staircase, they flashed, and every step was just right.

The impression I have is that she was dancing a tango, but she can't have been. There was no tango then, for her to dance. Something has superimposed itself, another image, some other woman dancing, later – ten years, twenty – a different one, in a different dress.

But close to me stood a fat Egyptian, his hands covered, and his teeth, in gold. And he watched her enraptured. And eventually he exclaimed, but not to me, although I heard him, "How beautiful she dances. Like a beautiful snake. Women are creatures of night."

CHAPTER TWO

Such Loveliness

Anna came into my room this morning.

She brought me a cup of tea, strong and clean-tasting, made from leaves not bleached bags, which addict you to the bleach, not properly to the tannin and caffeine.

The smell of tea, somehow, reminds me of the Nile, the swamps about the delta, something.

"Oh, you've been writing," says Anna, seeing the manuscript spread on my desk in the corner. I'm always writing, but Anna always remarks on it. Probably I mean her to, leaving the exercise books lying open, at the last page "May I read it?"

"Yes, if you want to. I don't mind. You don't have to read it."

"I'd like to," says Anna. Anna has always liked reading. Been rescued by reading.

Outside, the birds sing quite fiercely. The day is dark. A sullen, close, wintry summer hangs over London; the trees are thick with green, and the sky with cloud. The house is always dark, even at night, when the lights are switched on in some of the rooms.

From the house next door, to which this one is attached, comes a low-thumping heart-beat. Not the beat of the heart of the house, but of the music of the child of the house. The child is in its twenties. It is not very loud, but somehow the thing which is called beat – the heartbeat – of the music, comes in and under, through the floors and bricks. The child doesn't always play its music. Sometimes the child is in silence. And then they might all of them be dead.

The houses of this street are identical. Joined two by two, as if for the Ark. There are pointed roofs three storeys high. Victorian houses, with old, sequestered gardens. Old, near-to-dying trees, and leaning sheds.

In the bathroom, I wash my body and brush my teeth and use the shower attachment to cleanse my hair, which takes only a few minutes. I scarcely look into the mirror, here. I know who I am supposed to be.

Anna is downstairs, determinedly constructing breakfast. It smells very appealing. The meals of the day are small islands of cheerfulness.

Upstairs, he's quiet. I can't hear him. Usually I can't. The child with the music is more intrusive.

When I go down, careful, because of the pain, and the imbalance, I find Anna in the big kitchen. There's brown lino, or something like that, on the floor, and the walls are painted cream. The window looks out into the thick richness of the trees. Apples are on a bough preparing to rot. Anna used to pick them but can no longer do it. The same with the pear tree. She buys pears and apples at the corner shop. She has to tell him these are really ours, or he questions her: why do we waste the fruit on our own trees?

There's scrambled egg, with a toasted soft white roll, and some low-fat spread, to eat, but Anna has only one piece of toast, and even that is put by. First, she must take up his tray. He too has the eggs, on two slices of wholemeal toast, with butter. The coffee has to be made in his bedroom, or it will get cold, and he'll fret. Anna is already hurrying, not to let the eggs cool too much. Of course, I can't do this, I can't go fast or unclumsily, so Anna has to do it.

"You start, Esther," she says.

I must. The awful sinking is in my belly, and if I don't feed myself, soon I shall feel deathly sick. So I begin, cramming my mouth and body with the safe soft egg and almost safe roll. I pour more tea from the large pot, and then fill it again from the simmering kettle.

Anna will be gone at least twenty minutes. She has already been up once, heard his reports of the night, how he slept or didn't sleep. What he thinks of the day, what he wants. Now he'll be fully awake, and at his own table, and Anna will serve him his food, make the coffee. He'll talk about things, and about how wonderful she is, for looking after him so well, and she'll say, of course she would, what else?

When she comes down, her face is lost. I mean, she's lost her face, all expression, all identity. It comes back only slowly, and then probably it will be time to take him his midmorning tea and a biscuit. A plain biscuit. It must be plain. As in the afternoon, it must be more inventive. She spends a lot of time, finding him biscuits.

My plate's empty, like the rhyme. I could eat much more, but don't. Sometimes I allow myself also a small slice of white bread with marmalade. Not today.

I can note, from the exercise book lying on the worktop, that Anna has read quite a long way, in the hour I lay in bed, drinking the tea, waiting to see if I could catch up with myself.

Anna returns, to eat her cold slimy toast. I pour her tea and pass it to her. She says nothing for a while, during which her face tries to reassemble itself.

"He had a good night," she says at last.

He usually does have a good night.

"Yes," I say.

Anna says, "But I must ring the doctor, get him some more tablets." She makes a note on a piece of paper.

After this, she stops herself. She should maybe tell me all, repeat all he has said. Would this help her? Did she ever do this? Did I listen? No, I expect not, not either.

I thank her for the food, and say I liked it, which I did. The gloom that comes after a meal is already taking place, and I try to hold it away by making some more tea.

"I've been reading your story," says Anna. "It's so interesting. But you've used your own name. And mine."

"It's about me," I say.

"And – is it about our father?"

"Obviously."

"But…" says Anna. Again, she stops herself. Then she says cautiously, "But it's invented, naturally. The house in the story sounds very grand – I mean, at the beginning. The marble staircase the poor mother fell down, and the dew on the long front lawn."

I don't reply. The kettle is boiling. I pour water on fresh tea-leaves.

"You see, I don't *know*, but some of the details don't seem – quite right."

"Oh," I say.

"Paris – what you say about trams – I'm just not sure. Did you read something about Paris, then, in that era, to make certain?"

"No."

"Then it might not be right. Then, there's the French, the dialogue in French. It doesn't always look quite right. I'm no expert. But – well, the woman with the red hair talking about a dieting craze. This wouldn't have been that early. Nothing like that came in until – oh – 1920, I should think. And you mention neon, don't you?" She spreads her hands. "The earlier part too, in Egypt, it seems to be more than one place, your city. And you talk about the sea at one point, or was it meant to be later, in England?"

"Perhaps," I say.

"The Bugatti – did they make that car so early? You seem to put it at the turn of the century. And somehow, I don't know, little girls in *socks* – socks... That sounds more 1940's, somehow."

"You got so far," I say.

"I looked ahead. Your writing's so difficult to read. And all the ducks on the roof. And the tango – no, no. That was definitely in the 1920's – but it seems to be located much earlier."

"You've read to where I stopped."

"I'm afraid there were passages – your handwriting – I just couldn't make out. I had to leave them. It's not me, of course, the sister called Anna. Oh, I can see it's you, how you used to be. You'll change the names at the end, I expect."

"It won't be published," I say. "It won't matter."

"I know you went to Paris," she says. "But that was so much later."

"No," I say. "I went to Paris when I say I went."

"Did you? I don't remember your going."

"You don't remember our mother falling down the staircase?"

'Well, obviously I don't. She didn't."

"No?"

Anna looks, for just a second, very angry. Then she puts that away.

I replace the tea on the table and say, quietly, "Do you remember in Egypt, when the man had me against the wall, and was trying to finger me, and you took me off so politely, pretending *I* was being a nuisance, as if we were normal children and he wasn't a paedophile?"

"We were never," Anna says flatly, "in Egypt."

"I remember we were," I say.

"Oh really," she says. She laughs suddenly. "This is your new game, Esther? Well, why not?"

"Look at it like this," I say, "if we'd been children, and a man tried to molest me, that's precisely what you would have done, isn't it? Made a nice tactful excuse, and extracted me. Not risking violence by confronting him, not making a fuss. Keeping everything safe."

Anna lowers her eyes.

I again pass her a full cup, and then lift the lid off the pot. "Smell the tea," I say. "That's like the swamps around the river."

She looks at me softly. "I liked the bit about the women, the Muslim women, offering themselves to God."

"Do you remember the lemon blossom?" I say.

"*Is* there lemon blossom? Do you mean orange blossom?"

During the morning, between ten and twelve, Anna goes shopping. Sometimes I go with her, it depends how bad my balance is, my feet, my eyes. If I do go, I wonder what we look like. I try to visualise the two of us, but can't. Anna is very frugal and clever. She makes the money 'go round'. Our father's official pension, and the little extra amounts she has garnered.

I would guess people laugh at us. Does no one ever look and see, behind the horrible façade, two schoolgirls coping with their adult chores neither quite understands, but which we both are afraid of getting wrong. No, in fact, not me. I'm not afraid. I don't care. I would go and buy bread and cheese and wine, and I would let him starve, up there. I would feed the viper in my own stomach, and that would be that. But Anna must get it right. Just as, if she wrote a sentence in French, she would have to make sure it was absolutely correct.

At one o'clock, we have lunch.

We have salad, with bread for me, or omelettes. In the evening, Anna grills a chop for our father, or fish, or bakes steak and kidney pies, or quiches bought from the local store. We have eggs and chips, or tomatoes, or mushrooms on toast, or potatoes, which I fry with rosemary and olive oil.

At 12 p.m., I start to drink wine. I have a glass every hour, more or less. The wine is costly because it's quite good wine, though not any wine a connoisseur would recommend. I stop drinking after dinner, about 7.30. If I don't drink, usually I go blind. Or rather I see things that aren't there, stars, triangles and fireworks and merry-go-rounds of lights. This can happen anyway. But it's much less likely if steadily I drink wine. The condition is called migraine.

Here, I'll list all the things. It's tiresome. Could I avoid it? No, because then nothing will be explained, or rather, nothing will be true.

I'll start at the head, work down. I am subject to migraine visual attacks. These last half an hour to an hour. As I can't see physical reality during the course of them, I can't go out alone. There is no warning, but normally they attempt to occur every day or few days, and often two or three times in one day. There's no headache. But at other times, I have headaches, rather severe. Also, often, a black patch appears in my vision, now in one eye, now the other. Looking at a pale surface the black is sometimes blue, but red or white when looking at a dark surface.

Where next? Yes. In one ear, I have a droning noise that never stops. I don't notice it much by day, but at night I can't often lie on that side, as the sound is then so loud it seems deafening. I keep my radio on at night, for that, and other reasons. My back teeth are all metal, endless fillings painfully inserted and reinserted since childhood. These constantly break when I eat on them. Even chewing soft material – all I can manage – they have the feeling of tumbling bombsite walls. When I swallow food, something hurts, too, in my back. I'm so used to this that I scarcely notice it. But sometimes my stomach is sore. Sometimes, my lower stomach feels scalded; the wine eases this. But sometimes there is a feeling as if a boulder runs up my chest into my throat, and I must continually swallow this boulder, but it returns and returns. Sometimes there is a pain between my fallen breasts, as if I had been punched there with an iron stick. My stomach gnaws like a rat, gnaws at me, unless I eat pieces of bread between every meal, about every two hours. If I resist, I vomit.

My hip joints hurt, but only when walking, or occasionally when lying down. The bones in my feet, and my insteps are painful. And sometimes, altogether, walking is merciless, though not so bad, I imagine, as for the little mermaid, who walked on swords and knives, having lost her tail. In the mornings, my feet are like lumps of wood with springs of pain in them.

Often, I have vertigo. The world doesn't move, but something that is shaken loose in me. I have vertigo alone inside my own skull.

At night, every night, as I start to drift to sleep, a spasm suddenly wakes me too fast, and my body has stopped breathing. Instinctively, half aware, I start to fling myself about the bed to try to start the mechanism of life. After about ten seconds, I can breathe again. This happens over and over, every night, usually until I can no longer sleep. Frequently, my body refuses to sleep at all, that is to attempt to sleep, knowing what will happen to it. It lies resentfully, saying, Oh, no, *oh*, no. I hear a lot of world news this way. So, at last, the world has ceased to mean a thing. None of it is believable, as I'm catapulted back and forth, crowing for breath, dying for sleep. Every fourth, or fifth day, I do sleep for a few hours in the morning, generally after sunrise. I wake when Anna comes in about eight, and it *seems* that I have journeyed back from far away. Or, I *have*.

I can hardly recall a time when all this wasn't so. My earlier self is another person.

Now, looking in the mirror in my bedroom, I see this: A grossly fat woman, almost bald, and she too has lost her face, for the face is sunk into the neck of a white bullfrog, and her eyes are the eyes of a blind ghost.

Yes, she has seen doctors and dentists. Yes, yes. It is all so simple. This 'investigation', that. Things that, in Mediaeval times, would have been used for tortures, methods not to be considered. And drugs that cannot be taken. For example, the drug to control the spasms of waking and unbreathing causes – vertigo. The drug that would help the stomach triggers – migraine. The migraine tablets induce – weight-gain and nausea.

Poor thing. No, I won't look at her. Who is she?

"Father said," says Anna, as we drink tea at four, and I eat a slice of bread and margarine, "that he hasn't seen you for a long time."

"I saw him last week."

"Oh, *Esther*. You didn't."

"I did. I sat with him until he disappeared."

"Oh, *Esther*."

I had meant, my eyes had experienced another migraine. Anna doesn't understand. She forgets she helped me down the stairs, unable to see.

Or am I lying? Perhaps it was last month.

Upstairs, at the house's top, our father has his bedroom and his bathroom, both large rooms. At one end of his bedroom there is a library, one and a half walls lined with books. He only likes non-fiction, biography and travel, philosophical works by men of the eighteenth and nineteenth century.

As I enter the room, I see he is on the balcony that extends from the long windows of the room. He is a slim upright shadow, and beyond, the gardens, like a forest, our gardens and others in the street, extending to yet other gardens, and so to distant barely-glimpsed roofs. It might be anywhere that is luxuriant, the lowering sky gravid with rain, the opulence of the large and dull-green trees. But in the distance, a plane passes like a mosquito, curving round on what is called a flight path, robotic, foolish, a senseless automaton. Poor thing. It's full of people like germs, and may fall. Poor thing.

I am menstruating again – always irregular now – and this thing like a huge black thunder in my lower belly. A cheery doctor told me, women are currently so well-nourished, the menopause can certainly go on into one's sixties. Much is spoken of a young woman's glory in her flowering blood-rose womb. The spent blood smells like butchery, like murder – who tells you this?

My father turns.

"Esther."

He walks into the room, a tall man, with thick grey shining hair, brushed back, and the gold ring on his thin finger.

"I haven't seen you for so long. How are you? How you've worried me, with your illness."

"I'm better," I lie.

"Your sister is such a treasure," he says.

I have a sudden memory of Egypt. Anna ready for a dance in a silver dress. But we had come to England before that, surely. At thirteen, the gardener raped me in our English arbour, in that, other, grander, house. I know that our father thinks that our mother, the mother of Anna and myself, died of cancer. She didn't wear a flamey dress and fall headlong like a comet. It was in a cubicle, flat on a bed. But still, she was thirty-four. Or... was she forty-three?

My father sits and so do I, and I watch him with difficulty, for when there is a discrepancy of the light, as here, the half-shadow of his face dissolves. He has only half a face, and one bleak icy eye.

"Sometimes," he says, "when I go to sleep, I wonder if I'll wake up."

He can sleep. Oh God, he can sleep. Even Anna can sleep. The whole world can sleep. I see it sleeping, from my window. They say on the radio, at 5 a.m., Well, now's the time to make an early start – as if you had been sleeping sweet and deep, and woken to be virtuous.

My father is ninety. He doesn't look it.

"I'm concerned about Anna," he says. "She works too hard."

Half closing my useless eyes, I imagine running away. Fat and blind and bald and toothless, I see my body rummage through the world. But, on the cold hillside, I would not sleep. The noise in my ear wouldn't let me, and even if I didn't hear it, my brain would rouse me with a choking spasm.

"Such good daughters," he says. "I've been blessed."

I make tea in his room, and he's pleased, appreciative, commends me, as if I had passed a test. I get it right now, the slice of lemon, the strength of the Russian tea.

I recall him in a car in Egypt, and my mother under a vast hat.

But then I think of Paris, and the station – not the Gard du Nord – which station then? And how the night was there, and then I had to wait for a day, wait on the hard bench, and another man propositioned me, but an old woman came and interrupted us, wanting something, what could it have been? And I could only think of Julie.

When I go down, Anna is already starting to make the dinner. She is roasting a chicken, in which all three of us will join.

"How do you think he is?"

"He seemed well."

Anna looks glad, taking credit, and then dismayed.

"He's so gentle," she says. "He never recovered from mummy's death. It was such a shame." She bolsters him up. He was never harsh or unfair. He is noble, deserving.

All at once, the greyness of the sky beyond the kitchen window falters and lets through a stream of rose and fire. Anna stands up from the oven and we go to see, opening the back door, staring out down the stone steps, into the sea of trees and the aching rubicund sky.

"Isn't it lovely?" she breathes. "Such loveliness. Isn't that the truth of all of it? Nothing else. Or this is just an illusion – a *fake*. *That's* reality."

She and I renewed, seventeen, eighteen, on white wings, flying up into the rose sky. She and I, playing in heaven, light as dandelion clocks, telling the time of forever.

But another plane goes over on its *flight path*, spoiling the sky, and from the other house, the musicless music of the elderly child starts up. Nothing must be radiant, nothing must be left intact. The hymen of joy must be punctured. The womb of life must be claimed for misery and ten thousand *natural* shocks.

Poor Anna. So tired. Poor Anna.

"Let's have some wine," she says, as if I hadn't had any. And she opens a new bottle and fills two glasses.

CHAPTER THREE

The Dance of Death

The man bent over me in twilight. I knew what he wanted, and I thought it sensible to comply; besides I could ask for money, now I had learned how. Money had its uses.

But an old woman was there, she had a basket of flowers, and on their faces, hers dry and sewn like hessian, those of the flowers, smooth and purple, violet and white, rain or dew sprinkled.

She wanted us to buy her flowers. He would not, pushing her away, but she was wily, tough, and only cackled.

He kept saying to me, come on, he knew a place quite near. He would give me breakfast. And I remembered I must catch a train very soon, for it was morning now, and the twilight only the sky over Paris through the glass roof of the station. Or perhaps the roof was not glass, but it seemed to be.

So I said, "*Non, monsieur.*" And in English I explained that I wasn't a prostitute, he'd made a mistake.

At that he laughed. Of course I was. He didn't make mistakes.

The old woman thrust between us. She held the violets under my nose. And I smelled, through the station's smoke, how strange, English woods. I took the flowers and gave her a coin, and turning she said rapidly to the man, in French, something about how I always bought flowers from her, and I always waited here, on this day every month, to meet my sick mother from the country.

At this, he swore and looked down on me in rage, but put off. I said, "Her only pleasure, monsieur."

Just then, from one of the stopped trains, out of whose great

79

funnel smoke and steam still discharged, two railway porters emerged, and between them they carried a white stretcher, with someone lying on it under a blanket.

With surreal compunction I stood up, and the man, looking alarmed, unnerved, hurried away.

After he had vanished in the early crowd, the stretcher was borne by me, and I stared, quiescent, at an elderly woman, her face patient, terrified and sad, beyond embarrassment or prayer.

When she had gone by, the old woman with the flowers struck me lightly on the arm. She laughed soundlessly, and waddled away.

When the train arrived that was to be mine, I walked towards it without haste, carrying my bag, and the violets, through the rippling crowd. To me it was like a dream, and the train a creature of the dream, a huge animal of iron about which cinders flew like black moths.

What my wage had bought me was a seat in a long carriage upholstered in dark plush. Little grey curtains held back the panes of the windows.

I sat down, and put my bag beneath the seat and the violets in my lap. They would die on the journey, slowly crumpling into mauve-blue paper, perishing like everything which lives, but so swiftly, like butterflies, like minutes, too fast to mourn.

As a child, sometimes I wrote a diary, which I would allow Anna to read. She praised my writing but said that it was uncontrolled. Years after, I remember my father, hearing a woman screaming in orgasm from a room adjacent to our hotel suite, and remarking that she was so 'uncontrolled'. Of course, the only way to achieve the liberation of orgasm is to give up control. That is the entire point. I believe this to be true, also, of my writing.

And what do I recall of the journey? I ask this because, for example, I don't recall anything of my earlier journey from the port into Paris, I don't recollect where I came from. There was the sea, the episode with the sailor – and then, the city. But the journey towards the chateau, if it existed, if it was, took all that day, and all the night, and then some hours of the second day.

It was possible to buy food on the train, and in the end, I did buy something, in the dining-car, since I had just enough money. Some food, and a half bottle of some wine. I think there was a fruit I was given – an apple or a pomegranate.

But when I came back, a man had taken my seat, it was late at night, and in this carriage, everyone was preparing to sleep. I said to the man that he had taken my seat, and he made a shooing motion with his hands.

I went to the lavatory, and when I came back, he had gone. I don't know where, or why.

During the night, the world outside went by and it was not the world but a void. It was black, and lit only here and there, by some bluish lamp, or the light of some station at which we didn't stop. Or sparks flew back from the engine, like golden sequins. You sensed the blast of heat – like the *simoom* of Egypt, which Anna insists is called by another name.

Not sleeping, in that carriage where sleep was as thick as formulating cheese, I heard the snoring and the deep drowned breaths, I heard the murmurs of their dreams. Dreaming, they did so many things, those sleepers. Ran and fell, leapt from high buildings, sang in opera. And none of it was to be seen. The carriage lights had been put out, and the carriage was too dark. Now and then, outside, in the void, I saw distant openings that were supposedly the sky. But it could have been the backdrop revolving round and round, cunningly lit, while the train, in one place, rattled, and all done to convince anyone who stayed awake that we were really moving, really going somewhere.

But no one was awake, save I.

I looked at them. It would be easy to slink about, and slit the throats of most of them, as they slept, rob them, but then, here you would have to sit, amid the carnage, for the train surely *did* move, one could not jump off. This, at least, the bluff.

In the day before, the countryside had flowed by, it was green, there were lines of poplar trees, still bare, trees made of pale brown bones. Geese and pigeons, dovecotes, a flock of sheep on a winding road...

Where is it that I am? *Ou est* – where is – where is – Ouest. The west. The Land of the Dead.

People had chattered. They observed the rule, by day we must be, by night we must sleep. Was there no one in the whole train who had dozed as the light moved across the land of France, now pale, now congealed and almost gold, now with a band of pink, now blue, now gone. And then, at night, here in the heart of midnight or one o'clock, as they sat and sprawled, the fat woman with her head on the fat man's shoulder, the little clerk with his head tilted back, not one who was awake?

Suppose there were some obstacle on the line. A huge dray weighed by logs and drawn by horses of stone. And the train were to crash into it.

Thus in sleep, woken to death, thrown upwards in the air in a fountain of blood and amethyst sparks, the human screaming and the howl of the iron engine torn apart. I had reminded that man, so he said, of his daughter who died in a train accident.

Someone was awake after all. The man with the brown shoes. He smiled at me.

"And you had some fruit with your dinner," he said softly, in English. "I like to see that. It's good for the complexion, to eat fruit."

I sat, my head back on the plush, watching this man.

"Such a nice complexion, too." He took a watch on a chain from his pocket. "Two in the morning. The hour of the suicide. Would you like to come to the dining-car? They will give us brandy, or some hot milk. They'll do it, because I'll pay them to do it." He could not afford a sleeping-berth, but he could afford this.

"Non, merci."

"Ah, come now, what's wrong? Do you think I want something naughty? Well, you know I've heard, my cousin. He meets his mistress on the train, and has her in the lavatory. The motion of the train, you know. Very helpful."

I said in English, "I'd like to. But it's my mother. She's very ill. She fell down a stair. They don't think she'll live. That's where I am going, monsieur. To see my poor mother."

His face was white. He crossed himself. He said in French, "Ah, Gaston *warned* me…" and then he said, "Forget it," or as they say in French, *unremember* it. "Forget I spoke. Goodnight." And he shut his eyes and ran away into oblivion, to where I, with my rumours of death, couldn't follow. Or – perhaps I did.

Why did I refuse him? Hot milk in brandy, a childish comfort coupled to an adult one. Probably no payment, but a little gift, or, breakfast. But... no. No.

In the morning, first light, as I went out to brush my teeth and urinate, going through the corridor, a guard pushed me back sportively. He spoke only French. I thought I would have to, he was merry, insistent. But suddenly another man came, diverting him, he had to hurry away, pinching my cheek, regretful – apologetic – as if we had arranged to do it, and had been waiting a week, and besides, would meet later, and were friends.

I didn't bother with breakfast, but after we had stopped once or twice, I got a cup of chocolaty coffee with rich milk so thick it was like cream.

The countryside beyond the windows had changed, or been changed by the scene-shifters in the night. About eleven, the vista opened, fields, pastures, and I caught a glimpse of olive trees. They were yellowish-silver. And the sky was blue. The season had altered. It was warm, very warm. It was another country.

At the station, of which Agnes had told me, nine women sat in a row on a wooden bench. Each had a basket of eggs on her lap. Round the black skirts of all of them walked wonderful chickens, brazen-gold and red.

No one got on the train, or left it – save I. The women looked at me, without subterfuge, sitting on, and when I reached the edge of the platform, if such it was, the flat earth ran off into a lane, and this was all.

A man came, not in uniform, but for an official cap, a red scarf at his neck. He saluted me and I asked – *ou est* – for the chateau. He didn't understand me. Amused, he stood shaking his head. As I had once imagined, I had come into a land where I could not at all communicate.

Eventually I named the village. This puzzled him too. The way – partly Parisian, partly English – in which I pronounced the name, baffled him. Or apparently so. At last I asked just for the village – *le village*. Then he laughed, a great blast of laughter, and on the platform the women and the hens clucked in chorus.

He pointed. Down the lane. Where else?

Where, anyway, had he thought I meant to go?

In this new country, where I had just been born from the black womb of the iron train, the lane was hot and white with dust, and, as it turned right away from the track, full of deep holes, as if a giant beast had trodden up it not long ago. It was overhung by the summer-swollen foliage of trees, like heavy bunches of green grapes. I could smell fields, fields of things new to me, the grains and plants of another world. Bees hummed through the white flowers at the roadside.

When the village appeared, it lay at the bottom of a steep hill, and I could look down into it. There were russet roofs lying over each other like tortoises asleep. There was a public well in a square, and one street that climbed away with pink-washed houses, stacked like cards. Over walls spilled orchards. What strange fruit grew here? The grenadine, maybe, my pomegranate of the train. On a neighbouring slope, a brown child was herding white goats, I heard their bells. It was a picture from a book. But then, such pictures are inspired by such scenes.

Then I looked away, after the sun, and I saw the forest begin. I'd never seen such a forest, spreading and mantled, chestnut colour, nearly black, with lacy outcrops of green. Away and away it went, and on the edge of everything, a tracery of cloud that was not cloud but mountains.

Where had I come to?

A bird sailed through the sky. Was it a hawk?

There was a stone by the road. I sat on it and put down my bag. I still carried the Paris violets. They hadn't died, only they were very dry. I would slake them in some fountain, some well.

I shut my eyes. Birds sang and chirruped, a cricket or two scratched in the grass. The bees. It might be England. I might be in England, and this was my fantasy, that I was elsewhere.

When I opened my eyes, a cart was coming, drawn by a big-shouldered horse. The man paid me no attention until I stood up and approached. Not stopping the horse, he answered my question – Where is the chateau? – by – once more – shaking his head. He did not understand. Even so, he motioned to me that I could get up on the seat beside him. I did so with difficulty and the assistance of his hand; they didn't stop.

The back of the cart was full of cabbages and long broken boughs of fir trees.

As we rode into the village, he talked to me amiably. I didn't grasp what he said. He might have been telling me they would kill me there, and put me in a stew.

There was a bar facing onto the square, with an ancient grapevine curled all along its porch and down pillars that were made of tree trunks. Doves visited the vine constantly, pecking off single jade grapes and flying away with them. Card players and drinkers, men of course, sat beneath, and two women were by a well, each with two clean iron buckets.

Two dogs fucked diligently in a shadow at the entry to the street of pink-washed houses.

When the carter drew up in the square, there were cries of greeting and frivolity from the men by the bar. They motioned towards me, and I caught the words that perhaps referred to me. They seemed to describe me as a *sugar-girl*. Doubtless I didn't understand their accent and syntax, as they were immune to mine. The carter waved me off the box, jovial, like a kind uncle who had brought a child to a wished-for party.

Once I was down, he ignored me, left me standing in the square. He went straight into the bar, to a serenade of calls and congratulations.

I looked about. From three or four upper windows, narrow, with painted shutters flung wide, women gazed at me. All kinds of women, too, the young and fat, with firm juicy white skin, one thin and stern, one a brunette matron, handsome, with a fine black moustache she had not deigned to remove, and a golden ear-drop.

I called up to her, *"Chateau d'Ouest?"*

At this she laughed, raised her hands, gave me every indication that she could not comprehend a word – but she had enjoyed my performance.

Obviously, I could not walk into the bar. Here, not even a loose woman could do that. I turned round, and saw a serious-looking man walking down the pink street with a long-nosed black dog. It must have been a street for dogs, though the other two, the lovers, were by now gone. I waited, and as he came into the square, I went to him.

"Pardonez, monsieur…"

He jumped back in fright, and his dog growled. Even the dog refused to grasp what I said.

The man sidled past me and I let him go. On the terrace under the vine, the card players had reverted to their games. The women had gone in from their windows.

I crossed the square, and sat on a low wall, below which ran some open ground with a few fruit trees. If I kept still and silent, I believed they would forget me. I could sit until I toppled over and died. If I made no fuss, they would allow it.

And what now? Agnes had told me nothing beyond the area, and the name of the village – which, probably, was not even pronounced the same way, here. Could she have come here? Had it been her mischief to tell me? Or had her mischief been to mislead me? Despite what the evil red-head had let slip, to us both, the woods, the forests, the mountains, this place had nothing to do with Julie d'Ouest.

At the well, the women filled their buckets. I would not dare to attempt a drink of water, though, like the violets, I was thirsty. The sun beat on my head. I had no hat. Inevitably, this would be bad. I had always been told so... but that was Egypt.

A door banged. When I heard the steps, I turned cautiously. On the terrace, the men were laughing again, pointing at me. A shadow fell, and it was the woman with the moustache. Smilingly, she held by the hand a dark boy-child.

She said nothing, but the child, who was about seven, announced to me clearly, "I speak of the English."

I did not really believe it. But I said, "I'd like a drink of water, please. And then I want to know how to reach the chateau."

The boy looked up at the women and spoke rapidly, commandingly, in the village tongue. I think he called her Aunt. She nodded, let go of his hand, and went back to her house.

Alone, he stood before me. He wore trousers that had been carefully cut down, and braces, over a white shirt. "There is not any of the chateau."

It seemed to me that this was inevitable. The chateau was an invention of Julie's, and of Agnes'.

I said in French, "Perhaps, a big house..."

The boy shook his head irritably. He said, stiffly, actually unpleasantly, "You must speak with the English."

I repeated my suggestion in English.

"The big house," said the boy, "lies there. A road goes between the woods. The house waits by the road." One of the men, watching in glee from the terrace, called something to the boy. The boy said to me haughtily, nastily, "There are boars about the forest,"

"Wild pig?" I asked.

He was blank. With disdain, he assumed I meant to catch him out. He said, coldly, "Stay to the road."

After this he turned, applauded by the men, and marched to the house and went in. The woman returned, though, with a white pitcher and a cup. She gave me the water I'd requested, and watched me drink. I put the violets into the cup with half the water left in it, and handed both to her.

To my astonishment and discomfort, she curtseyed. She carried the cup, pitcher, flowers, reverently into her house. The door was shut. In ten years she would be aged, by the standards of the village, and the horrible child would be a man. He would sit at the head of the table, and mock her as she brought him her glorious cooking, as she cleaned his boots. Soon a young wife would be added, fawning and sly. He would stalk in, flinging dead hares, birds caught in snares, on to the table. The girl would elbow the old woman aside, and rule the roost until she, too, ruined and distended with child-bearing, would lose her place, and some beastly little son would stamp across the rooms.

How had the brat learned English? Such bad English and so easily understood.

As I stood up, blood rushed through my head. I had a momentary vision of the woman of the station communing with the matron of the moustache. Perhaps I had only come here to give the violets. Perhaps they were a signal. She would go to the train and travel to Paris, paying for her fare with money stolen for years from father or brother. They, the old flower-seller and the matron, would meet and totter along the boulevards, raucous, uncouth, dreadful and magnificent. Or she might eat the violets and grow young again. So beautiful, they would have to pay her attention. But probably, she was proud of the horrible child, probably thought it her crowning glory, to tend the men of the house, to please them. And their jibes and discourtesies were lost on her.

I walked dazedly through the village, my bag in my hand. The houses passed, and the functional gardens thick with plants, peas and apple trees. Three yellow pigs snuffled over the path, and beyond was the road through the woods.

It was so like some fairy-tale – Red Riding Hood, presumably, I felt a new purpose.

Agnes had said there were no longer wolves, but that was her village near Paris, only six hours away by cart.

The trees went up, seeming prehistoric in their magnitude, their density, their thick green shade, the smell of mulch, endless cycles and returnings.

To walk through the forest then was to walk through the body of a thing part dead, part living, part in labour.

The green of its recesses was a different colour. It had the richness of mature metal, and the delicacy of fresh lettuce. And there were tunnels of dark blood. There you saw the bones of the wood, the sinews, enormous muscles, veins.

I was amazed by it, in a stupid way. To me woods were slender things, with copses of bluebells, the magical myths of 'home'. There are in Egypt only forests of stone. And yet, this forest was like that, the pillar-crammed temples of the Nile. Even the trees had a sort of writing on them. And, as with the hieroglyphs, I couldn't read it.

The smells of the forest were in keeping with the rest. Salad smells of new growth, and the stink of corpses. Here and there a dead creature, picked almost clean. And the feathers of birds scattered like snow.

It was early in the year. Although I had passed from spring to summer in a night, yet it was not – not summer. Spaces showed in the canopy above which, by July or August, would be black tapestry.

I kept to the road. Not that it was a road. A type of track, in parts vanished under moss and grass, or a tree fallen across it.

A flash of blue, and an incredible bird like a gas-jet, spurted from one tree to another. Sometimes, the birds sang, but at my arrival they fell silent, or clamoured.

Why on earth was I walking in this labyrinth? If I went off the path, I'd be lost for ever. And maybe the path would cease.

The house wouldn't exist, or it would be a ruin. At best, it wouldn't be the house that Julie or her sister had mentioned.

For hours, I walked. I think it was for hours. A stream ran by the path, thin green as vitriol. In a more open place, rosemary bushes filled the air with their herbal scent, bloomed with bees. I saw a dead abandoned honeycomb hung on a tree, like a grey skull.

Afterwards, if I told anyone about this travelling through the forest in France, they refused to believe me, and so perhaps, the chateau only lay off the road, just beyond the village. Memory alters. As when you recall some passage in a book with utter clarity, and later, reading the passage again, find it goes differently, the words reversed or the image, the character not the same one you thought, or else the scene occurs in another place. Or another book.

The light began to slant. It was long after noon. Shafts ran sidelong down through the parasols of the branches, the large chestnuts and cedars, and through the skeins of wild vines. In a shadow, dense and brown as a wardrobe, I paused to rest. And then the boar came, cantering down an avenue between the columns of the trees.

Could he see me, this awful engine of violence? He was not so very big, but like a barrel on legs, his enormous head in its helmet of bristle and tusks, swinging from side to side. His eyes were black, with red outer rims. Close by, he stopped, snuffed up the air of his wood, and caught the scent of me.

Between his hind limbs his organ pointed out. It looked deformed, like the weapon of pigs. He rubbed his tusks on the trunk of a great black tree, already scarred and rent, presumably by him.

Shaken by his strength, the young leaves dropped like primrose confetti from the boughs above.

If he came to me, could I diffuse his murderousness in the usual way? The ancient Romans had tied Christian women in the arena, their legs pulled wide, smearing them with the appropriate liquors, and lions and boars had mounted them, bursting them before the cheering crowd.

But he wouldn't be so hard to manage, not really. Would I have to do it? Would he accept it from me, as men had done, piercing me, spending their strength in me, rather than beating me, killing me?

The boar lifted its head. He was all head, head and penis, borne on four stout little legs. He trotted mildly away.

When I came from the shelter of my tree, I could smell him, dark and meaty, the odour of a minotaur, undeniably male, yet formed from the earth and the soil of the forest out of which he had erupted, not birthed in the usual fashion.

No one believes the story of the boar. Possibly I was nervous and simply envisaged such a thing happening, and how I might escape. I remember it exactly as my own name, and every bristle on his side, his ivory tusks, his black mouth from which raindrops of saliva dripped.

I found the gateway when the light was becoming syrupy and the shadows very long. There was a running, partly broken, high wall, and two gate posts, on each side of which bulbed a blackened glass lamp, and round which ivy had rooted. The gates were of black iron with chips of gilding still on them, like something that might be seen in a city, on a civic building or a justiciary. One gate hung open, listless. Less inviting than uninterested. You might pass – who would care?

Beyond, a wide drive, thick in last year's brown leaves, and with limes, I think, on either side, many of which had mostly died. Yet all were full of nests, and birds flew over and back, finches, and black birds with slits of red on their wings.

As I walked up the drive, the ground sloped over, and I saw the big house, which was not a chateau, more a kind of farm dwelling, but large, with a pair of towers. Behind it the sun was westering. Yes, the house stood against the west, which was tarnished golden. And on the sky's hem, the mountains, like an etching on glass, transparent.

Around the front of the house was a lawn which had run wild to everything, flowers, weeds, bushes, and across it rose a dancing line of ancient olive trees. There was a fountain too, a greened basin out of which stood a stone girl, hiding her breasts and her sex with her hair.

I thought dogs would bark as I approached, and one did. But it wasn't the proper barking of hounds, or guard dogs. Excitable, too light.

Scorched shutters stood back from the windows in which there was glass, but nothing else to be seen. Getting closer, I noticed, behind the house and between the house and the sky and the mountains, fields striped saffron yellow in the dropping sun. And plantings of more olive trees.

Not a thing moved, but for birds, and the imperceptible declining of the slow sun. There was one cloud, like a mountain thrown up in the sky. This too was still.

A terrace extended along the house front. There were two steps to a door. It looked solid and stiff, as if it could never be opened.

The dog had left off yapping.

I went by the fountain, which had no water, only the modest girl, and stopped in front of the shallow steps.

Roses grew over the terrace. Their buds were small and meagre and their thorns primed like unsheathed claws. It was a strange house, not right in any way, its architecture, its personality.

Would I knock on the peculiar knocker, shaped like a lyre? And to all those rows of windows, would any face come?

I stepped back. I began to count the windows. Thirty, it seemed to me on the upper floor, and then, in the attic above, the towers, perhaps only eleven or twelve.

The light of the day's last quarter streamed round the sides of the building and over the roof and the two short towers, and straight through the window in one tower, like lamplight.

A dove cooed from behind the house.

The obdurate door grunted, and was pulled open.

There she stood, that bizarre little girl from the doorway in Paris, her foggy curly hair coerced into a bushy plait, a white pinafore over a black dress, and her feet bare and brown and cruel as the feet of a bird.

She grinned. She said, "Come in, come in."

Had she spoken in English then? Did she now?

I said, "What's your name?"

"That would be telling." She skipped back, and I saw beyond her, inside, a shadowy large chamber, with one pillar standing up, like the hollow of a temple.

At the back of the house, and one whole storey lower, was a colossal kitchen. The light had been exiling itself, and everything else went by, not properly to be seen, half or completely masked. But down these stairs the child led me, and out into this huge room. The floor was of stone flags, each some three feet square. Here and there one had raised itself a little – a treacherous floor, unless you were very used to it. The walls were of old reddish plaster, beautifully patched and discoloured and in parts cracked, revealing seams of sandiness. One might linger here, and find faces or monsters or maps in them. From a low-beamed ceiling hung vegetables, copper and pearly white onions, tomatoes drying randomly on cords of malachite stem. There were three narrow windows, each the colour of Sauterne from the compressed day sky, but set high up, and nothing more than light was visible. Nothing. The kitchen was adrift as a boat.

Cupboards, shelves, a vast scrubbed table of whitish wood – the kind on which the child is laid to be operated on in the garish novel, at midnight – appendicitis – or the woman unlawfully pregnant, for delivery. On such a stony floor their blood, in fiction or fact, had poured, and doubtless the black carnivorous mice crept from their holes to sample it and be nourished.

But the room was ruled over by the great fire-place that ran almost the length of one long wall, and had stacked itself nearly to the ceiling. It was faced with blood-orange brick, and hung with drying herbs in switches, like the tails of witch brooms, more tomatoes that ebbed into its colour, ancient pans of dark iron, black torture instruments that had to do with basting and turning food. Inside the hearth ran black lines of metal, spits with chains for the rotation of carcasses, griddles for baking. A large brown jar stood at the border, a sentry, with its halberd, a toasting fork, leaning on its hip. There was no fire in that hearth. It was Hell, after they had doused the lights, armoured in grease and particles of the roasted damned.

A tall straight-backed chair, old as the eighteenth century, bulked out from the edge of the monstrous fireplace. In it sat a woman, bolt upright, in a long and voluminous old-fashioned skirt, the sheen of the light over her amassed grey hair, and the dog, Henri, seated in her lap. It was a definite impression I had, the chair itself seated, and the woman seated *in* it, and the dog seated on her knees, all as upright as the seating posture will allow.

Henri it was – was it – who had barked? That silly hysterical quacking of a small pampered lap-dog, who, if need be, would probably die with just the same honour as a wolfhound, to defend his mistress. He no longer made a noise. He looked at me complacently: Oh, it's only you again? And the child with foggy hair had gone at once to a stool near the table, and sat herself there. From a dish of berries, she began to select individual fruits, popping them into her mouth with avid enjoyment.

The old woman was thin and hard, corseted in her own bones. Unlike the beastly red-head who had had Henri last, she gave off no aroma. And the kitchen smelled strongly of earth, fungus, onions, bread, soot and bitter honey.

"Well," said the old woman. "So here you are." She spoke in English, but very slowly, and with an accent that filled her mouth, crowding the words, but not smothering them. "Number Thirty-Four."

I stood on the flagstones in the lamplight of late afternoon. I said, "What do you mean, madame?"

"*Grand*madame," she said, sternly. "That is what you must call me. Grandmadame. And you – you are Thirty- Four."

"No," I said. "If you mean my age, that's twice my age. What *do* you mean?"

Henri, lifting his eyebrow, turned about a couple of times, like a cat, and lay down. In the light, he was an anaemic nasturtium shade. He looked very much like a pig.

"Sit," said the woman, the Grandmadame. She gestured to the child, "Fetch forward a chair."

The child obediently got up, dragged a chair from the table, a more ordinary chair, perhaps only a hundred years old, and put it for me, facing the inquisitor.

"Sit," said the Grandmadame again. "You walked from the village – is that not so?"

"Yes."

"Sit you, then. Sit, sit."

I sat. I said, frankly, "Where is Julie D'Ouest?"

The old woman moved her hands on the arms of the chair.

She had a big ring on one finger that caught the light. It might be a ruby. "So many times," she said, "this scene. They come before me, in their city frocks, fainting from weariness, mad with love. All for him. All for my son."

"Your son," I said.

"My Julot," she said. At her naming of this name, not quite the one I'd been given, the dog beat briefly with his tail.

"Your son," I said again.

The child, who had gone back to her berries, emitted a vile little giggle. I thought of the house of the red-head, and this child, and how she had shut me up and pretended to burn me. And that had apparently happened to many young women. How many? How many of them had discovered Agnes? And so... foregathered here?

"Oh," said Grandmadame, reading my mind, "they don't all come. Not all. A few. Five or six. Or seven. Or ten. I forget. All the same. The same little girls."

"So," I said, "thirty-four little girls haven't come here?"

"No, that is the other number." Grandmadame shifted a fraction. The light described her face. She was an elderly country woman, a peasant, with a mass of strong and wiry hair in which some strands of jet black remained. Her eyes were also black. And in her sunken cheeks, the broken veins, that once had been a high and flaming colour, painting her like a flower. Julie...grown old? Not quite. Yet, it was there. "You will understand," said Grandmadame, "my son must go to the city of Paris. It has to do with the business of our land. And he will go three times in every year. And every time, even now if he takes the child, he leaves her with the other. And then Julot finds for himself a young woman. For eleven years this has gone on. And so, there have been thirty-three he has seduced. And now, in the twelfth year, he goes to Paris again, and you are the result."

Which made me, evidently, Number Thirty-Four.

I looked down at my hands on my bag in my lap.

Grandmadame said, "Why he must do it is a mystery to me. But they are both mysteries. He and the other one."

I said, cautiously, "Your son's sister?"

"Brother."

I shut my eyes. Let me get it right. Yes. Grandmadame made pretence that Julie was a man – just as Julie made pretence of it.

And Julie's red sister – was therefore a man, too, presumably. A *brother*. And the child?

"This one," I said, "to whom does she belong?"

Grandmadame said, "Julot's daughter."

I laughed. It was as vile and unpleasant a sound as the giggle of the child.

"Well," I said, "it's very kind of you to be so forthcoming."

"What is this *forthcoming?*"

"Your honesty."

"Poof," she said, as the red-head had, "why should I not tell you the truth." She spoke to the child in the language of the region, what I had heard them speak in the village. The child rose, fetched a jug from the cupboard, and poured a blue cup full of milk. This she brought me.

"We have not poisoned it," said the Grandmadame.

"No. Why should you?"

"Because you may be a pest. But we will put up with you, Thirty-Four."

I drank the milk. It was sour, turning, yet still cool and refreshing.

The child began noisily to set the table with plates and knives and spoons, and condiments in dark brown jars, and a salt cellar that was silver, with a little animal on the top, where, by twisting, you must grind the salt down to powder.

"My name's Esther."

"No. Here you are Thirty-Four. I say it in your English, to be fair to you. But you'll get no more than that."

"So, I'm Thirty-Four. And you are Grandmadame. And what is she?"

"The child. Call her *the child*.

I pointed at the dog. "But *he* has a name. Henri."

"Oh," she said, "the other calls him that, my red son, my horror. My beast."

"I met a beast on the way to your house."

She glanced at me. I saw her black eyes flash.

I said, "A great boar."

"No, there are no boar in the forest now," she said. "They were hunted out."

"But there are wolves," said the child, sing-song, as she pranced round the scrubbed table with a loaf of sulky darkness and burnt crust.

"No wolves, no boar," said Grandmadame. "When I was a girl, oh yes. Those wolves would come to the edge of the lawn, in winter. They were thin as ghosts." She added, "You see this pig?" She poked the dog.

"Henri?"

"The pig, the pig. What do you think he looks like?"

I shook my head.

"No, you are quite well aware. He looks like a pig, a pig with hair on him. There were dogs kept then, and one day a boar got hold of a bitch in her – what do you say – her hot blood. And the boar had her." She squinted at me. She said, precisely, "Fucked her, with his evil pizzle. And when she had the litter, there were three dogs and this one, this pig. What do you say to that?"

I said, quietly, "You've a son who's a daughter and a daughter who's a son. Why not a dog who's a pig?"

As I said this, my heart turned to rock. It was hard and silent, stricken – for what could she do? I could imagine her, this malevolent beldame, springing at me, squeezing to a rag my neck in her hands, all knuckles and ring.

But she dismissed me, lifting her big old nose. "What nonsense you talk. You should have been born in the country. You see things, there."

"In Egypt," I said, "I saw a man run a knife through his arm, and pull it out the other side. There wasn't any mark, and no blood."

She looked interested. But then she said, "Some trick. There are always those." She got up. It surprised me, her smallness. The dog-pig leapt to the floor and then jumped up on the stool by the table where the child had sat. "You may eat with us," said the Grandmadame.

So we dined, the matriarch, the child, the dog or pig, and I. We ate the black bread, spread with thick green olive oil, chunks of tomato and slices of nacreous onions There was a pitcher of icy water to drink, from a spring or well. It was sweet and metallic together.

"It will be too simple for you," said Grandmadame, "but here, we do not live like royalty."

In the windows, the sky was now intense with gold, and birds fluttered over again and again, casting fluttering shadows like flickers of thoughts.

"I could put you out, to sleep in the forest. What would you do if your boar found you? They will take a bitch dog. Why not a little bitch of an English girl?"

I didn't reveal what I had considered before. I didn't say that I had already been had by wild boar, in the gardens and alleys and sunny rented rooms of England.

Henri ate olive oil and onion and tomato and bread, cut or mashed for him by the child. His nose shone with the oil and there were tomato seeds around his muzzle, but he was far more decorous than he had been with the cakes in Paris. His mood had changed. Perhaps truly he was half pig.

After her threat about the boar, the harridan stopped talking to eat. I compared many aspects of the meal with the other meal, in Paris, with the red-headed one. Both times, there had been chat of poison. Something occurred to me, made me pause. Could it be that the red-head actually was a man, a man clad as a female, as Julie clothed herself as a male? The clipped voice assumed? The appalling female stench he had perhaps applied, with his cologne.

Dusk gathered in the vault of the kitchen.

Above, the rest of the house creaked and sang to itself. This was an evening that might go on and on.

After our dinner or supper, the child told us a story. It was Little Red Riding Hood in essence, except that the wolf ate her alive as well as the grandmother.

Children irritate me, they always have, I don't know why. At seventeen, in that situation, I was doubtless more exasperated by the child than I would have been otherwise. Her stupid, self-opinionated voice, ignorant, of necessity, putting the wrong emphasis on every third or fourth word – and yet, she had a total command of English. She had not asked to tell her tale, merely launched into it, like a valued entertainer sure of her role. And the Grandmadame – the grandmother – listened respectfully, consideringly, the way an adult should to an aspiring child.

When the story ended, the Grandmadame said, "So, they

were eaten."

"Yes," said the child. She tossed her plait.

"And serves them right," said the Grandmadame, "for their silliness."

It had become dark now. Over the open land outside an owl called and another answered it.

"Prepare the chocolate," said the Grandmadame to her granddaughter. "I will light the lamp."

This she did, a big oil lamp which had the colour, when lit, of the afternoon.

The child meanwhile was grating a big slab of black chocolate into a pan above a spirit-lamp.

Grandmadame nodded to me. "We seek our beds early here, and rise early. The chocolate is not for you," she added maliciously.

"I thought it was for you."

"No. For another. Ah, not for Julot. Julot is not here. Not yet." She waited but I did not reply. She said, "The chocolate is for Julot's wife."

What could I say? I said nothing. If Julie was a man, a son, why not a husband too?

The child stirred the chocolate, poured it into a cup on a saucer, added a little of the turning milk, stirred the concoction and was ready.

Out of the kitchen we went, and up the steps, Grandmadame leading with her light, the child and chocolate next, then myself, and lastly Henri, snuffling. A flock of shadows also accompanied us.

In the tunnel of the lamplight, I saw now the open hall above, with its one tall pillar, which seemed to uphold the ceiling. On a wall was a shield, antique, with faded magenta triangles on a dull ochre ground. A little wooden stair went creeping up in a corner behind a door that stood ajar. Up this in turn we went.

We progressed into a corridor, which came out suddenly on a bizarre open gallery. Below, the hall we had just passed through, and the pillar, but on the wall at our side, when the lamplight found it, some disgusting Mediaeval fresco, or copy of one, very crude, of many people, with the ugly mindless faces of another time.

Grandmadame paused, and raised on high her lamp.

"Look," she commanded. We looked, the child and Henri too.

The picture was set in a garden or orchard, for here were fruit trees with round, hard reddish fruits. The women wore long gowns of faded blue or pink, big-bellied, their headdresses like cows' horns. The men stepped in strutting poses, their legs, and genitals, caught in cod-pieces, indecent and boastful, since they were the lords of life. They were dancing, these beings, for a piper led them, and a drummer, and another with a fiddle. But the musicians were naked, naked to the bones, skeletons. At the procession's head capered Death, robed in brown, beckoning them all to come on.

"You see," said the matriarch to me.

"The Dance of Death."

"It is the old wall of the house," she said. "We keep it. It was done after the Plague."

The child shivered. But it was not death she was afraid of, only the spectres.

"Now," said the Grandmadame to the child, "it is nothing to fear."

The child turned, careful not to spill the chocolate, and looked deliberately away.

"Go on to your mother now," said Grandmadame. "Look, there is her light."

Beyond the gallery, another lamp was burning at the end of another corridor, warm and welcoming. The child sidled past the wall painting, and hurried down the corridor. The dog-pig hopped after her, wagging his tail as he passed beneath the figure of Death.

"But we go another way," said the Grandmadame.

She led me up into the attics, familiar route. But apparently I was only to sleep here; there was a bed in this room, and even an antiquated, though perfectly operational, cabinet for night soil.

The bed had been made up, perhaps it always was, for the next girl of Julie's who reached the house. Had it even received into the same sheets, on the same bony pillows, every girl, and nothing changed or washed, so the sweats and perfumes and sighs of every one were mingled, their texture by now as thick as the quilt?

On a chest stood a basin and a jug with water, a dry cake of soap, a folded towel, a fat candle, a box of matches. There was also a large oval mirror on the wall, and suddenly Grandmadame and I, bathed in the radiant roar of the lamp, were duplicated in it. She was shorter than I was, yet she still seemed tall. And I – was like a shadow, skin shadowy waxy pink from the lamp-glow, eyes huge and dark, dark as her eyes, but not so miraculously hard.

"Thank you for the bed," I said to her, coldly.

She said, "There is more."

In the far wall, the wall that had been dwarfed by the slope of the roof, was a window, I crossed to it and looked out – instinctive action of the prisoner – but, with the light, I couldn't see anything, except maybe the tops of the forest – that forest, any forest.

"No, not there," she said.

She beckoned me, and when I didn't respond, she went to the chest, took off all the implements, basin and jug, towel, candle, matches, soap, putting them on a small table with her lamp. She then raised the top of the chest, which was it seemed a lid. "Come and see."

What did I expect? The skeleton of a child laid on satin, a mummified animal, or even a baby. Oh yes, any of those. But I thought it would be letters, in fact, in bundles. Love letters written to Julie. Or even letters from lunatic asylums to which these thirty-three other discarded paramours had been assigned – all but one: Agnes.

But when I approached and looked down into the chest, there was plain wood, and set in to it a round hole. The hole contained a perfect vignette, rosily lit. A young woman lay on pillows and a little girl beside her, in her arm. I thought it a curious life-study, another picture, until the dog ran up the bed and nudged into their embrace.

"How is it managed?" I said.

"A spy hole. Arranged long ago for one who liked to watch but not to do."

The dog barked, and they stilled him, the woman and her fog-haired child.

"If we can hear them, can't they hear us? Can't they see us?"

"A trick of mirrors and tubes. There is an old chandelier in that room. This thing is hidden in the fitting. If you shouted at them they would hear. Do I tempt you? This below is my son's room, the bedroom he shares with his wife. And there she is. Thérèse. With their child."

"So *she* has a name."

Grandmadame said nothing to that. Had she let the name slip? Surely not. It was another obscure but pure malice. Julot's wife, like Julot, had a name. His child, his dog, his brother, his mother – and all his random mistresses – *none.*

Why did she want me to look at this?

"Why are you showing me?"

"So you may see."

I saw. The wife of Julot – Julie – was pale and slim, with long soft dark-honey-coloured hair. She wore a nightdress trimmed with dull lace and ribbon. The child wore something similar. They murmured to each other, of course in French, I couldn't catch the words.

It would be easy to spy on love-making in this bed. By moving a little, one could see most of the surface. That had been, anyway, the spy hole's purpose.

Grandmadame had sidled off. She took up the lamp.

She said nothing, opening the door of the room and going out. The door closed, the light had gone. She did not lock me in.

The only light now soaked up from the aperture inside the chest.

I leaned over, and listened.

Something happened. Not only that I now heard clearly, which might be simply the skill of the tubes, and the acoustics of the chest, but again, I heard the French and understood it, as I had with Agnes. Possibly what I understood now was not true. And might this also have been the case with Agnes...

Thérèse, the mother, was in her turn telling the child a story. It sounded familiar, and for this reason then, I thought, I began to follow it.

"The goddess searched all over the world for her lost love. She went from city to city. No one knew her, because she had cut her hair and put on a dress of mourning."

"Was it black?" asked the child.

"*Couleur d'hiver*... It was the colour of winter. But from her, from her skin, came a beautiful smell. Because she was a goddess."

"*You* smell beautiful," said the child in a passion, snuggling close.

A strange thing. A sharp pain in my eyes, and tears bursting through, horribly, really, like pus erupting from a boil. The smell of the mother you have loved. Did I remember it? It seemed so. Perhaps she does smell sweet. But it's love that makes the smell of her into magic. That then is the secret of the wondrous perfume of the goddess, mother, and lover.

"Poor goddess," said the woman, Thérèse, whose colouring was so like mine. "She asked them all – have you seen my daughter, my child, with her golden hair?"

The child simpered. Her hair was not gold, it was an awful shade: London smog. However, to the loving mother, gold, perhaps. And, if constantly she named it gold, might it become like gold?

And no, the child did not simper.

The child – was happy.

"But not one had seen the daughter of the goddess, the daughter who had vanished away into the ground," said Thérèse, Julie's – wife.

They lay against the pillows in silence, thinking of this. The child would be imagining it, how she had picked a flower in the forest or field, the ground had opened wide, and she had fallen in, where a dark being had seized her, carried her off in his black chariot.

And did Thérèse think how she would follow her child, searching for her?

The dog, too, was slumped and mute.

"She came, the goddess, to a city, and the daughters of the queen found her. They were astonished by the luminescence that broke from her, and the scent of her. They took her to the queen, who hired her at once as a nurse for her own child."

The daughter of Thérèse looked up at this, rapt.

Thérèse said, "Now, she didn't give the child milk. No, she breathed on him her divine essence. And then she would lay him in a brazier of flame to burn away his mortal part and make him like a god."

The daughter of Thérèse said, "But if she set fire to him, she'd kill him."

"Ah, no. Because she was a goddess, you see. And when she'd done this, all she could, the goddess Demeter sat weeping for her daughter."

It was the story of Demeter, the Greek or Roman goddess of the corn – like Isis, a deity of agriculture. Her daughter had been stolen from her, not her husband. Substantially the same, however. These goddesses both searched the world over. And finding the child of a queen, nurtured it by burning it alive. And both were interrupted.

"The queen rushed in, screaming. She snatched her baby from the brazier. Then Demeter revealed herself, and explained what she had done. After this, she left the palace."

"Did she find her daughter?" asked the child of Thérèse.

"Yes, of course. But that's for tomorrow. Now, we must sleep."

They lay further back in the rosy bed. For a moment, it seemed to me that they too lay in the flames, in a brazier of softest light. But then their lamp, probably at the mother's touch, went out.

All was darkness.

I let down the lid of the chest, crept to my candle, lit it. My eyes, how dry they were.

When I returned to the window, the stars shone bright above the forest of France. The French owls called like spirits.

I haven't spied, eavesdropped, very often. The other time, which naturally came back to me that night, was when I hesitated outside the door of my father's study, in Egypt, at Number 12, rue Des Palmes – the street of hands.

Why did I?

The *simoom* – or *khamsun* – was blowing, and the shutters were closed. My mother lay on her bed, with the cold cloth on her forehead steeped in lavender or some other herb. Anna played Chopin, picking, stopping, stumbling. Once in a while, she would achieve a brief fluid passage, redolent of feeling, expression, and expertise. This would last, at most, for two or three bars. Then she would stumble again, and again begin to pick about, as if she had gone suddenly blind in the midst of a known place which she, along with most of the sighted, could only identify with her eyes.

The light was gloomy, reddish, tinted by the febrile wind. Afternoon? Beyond his door, I heard him say, "I confess it. I'm afraid it could kill me."

What did he mean, my father, to me? He was like the bedrock, the wall which held us all inside some sort of castle. Had I formed this image about his strength, or had my mother done it? And Anna, too. No doubt, Anna too. How old were we then, she and I? Ten, eleven, twelve... No older. We were gone from Egypt after that.

I felt very small, lightweight. I stayed by the door.

Through it I heard the laugh of Mr Golden – the friend from the shrine, Mr Golden of the car and the flask and the wife with hats and crossed eyes.

"Come now. *No.* Well, what symptoms do you have?"

"My father had it." My father too, amazingly, had had a father. "He died of it, obviously. After they had – you know what's done."

"My God, yes. But don't think of that. It isn't that."

"Passing water. It's difficult. And, there's blood."

"Have you been with a woman?" A silence. Mr Golden said, "I know what it's like. My Miriam is wonderful. But sometimes... there's the teasing way they move, here. And that look."

"No, I haven't done that."

"Listen," said Mr Golden, "I know a doctor. No, wait. He's very good. An old Jew. Clean as your sheets. He'll understand."

"I've thought – of blowing out my brains," said my father's voice. "I won't be brought to it. To have that done to me. To end – like that."

"Come and see him, my old Jew. He's a marvel. I'll tell you. I had a problem once. But he cleared it right up. It's nothing. It's the filthy water here. That river is full of shit."

I stole down the corridor and came into the guest bedroom, where I levered the shutter open. Outside and below, the cook sat under his awning by the kitchen hut. He smoked a cigarette and the reddish wind blew by.

Would my father die, then? Would my mother, after this,

wander the streets of the city? Would she have to wear a veil? If I told Anna, Anna would be afraid. Anna would try to protect me. It would be too much for Anna.

I didn't care. I visualised my father dead, my mother, Anna and I, freely drifting about the city. Nothing would be certain. We would eat crusts or mashes of grain in bowls. Perhaps thieve and run away. What did it matter?

In the evening, the wind dropped. Anna came in and found me, sitting by the window. I said to her, "Father's going to die." I don't know why I did. Conceivably I had forgotten my resolve not to mention it, or dozed and dreamed she knew, it was an established fact. Or did I want to frighten her? But Anna said in a whisper, "So you know. It's a blockage." I stared and asked her what this meant. She shook her head.

Long after, years, by some roundabout route, she had discovered all the event and its outcome. Our father had had trouble urinating and blood had issued from his member — however did she hear of this – from our mother? He was terrified that it was a terminal blockage, what has come to be recognised as cancer of the prostate – from which his own father had died. Nevertheless, jolly Golden persuaded him to the 'old Jew', who examined him and assured him that the ailment was only a minor infection, which indeed was soon cured by infusions which the doctor prescribed. Our father was never troubled again in this way. And so, unlike the story of Osiris, the crab did not devour his penis.

Dawn came through the attic window, which faced east. It was as golden as the sunset had been, but sheer, without density, as if the sky was only light.

Birds sang, even a cock crowed, and the doves that later I found roosted behind the house, flew up and down. What a wonderful morning, Anna would have said. Anna, always so dutifully responsible, so oppressed, and so ready to snatch at the joy of life, quickly, utterly, before it could escape; as always, soon enough, pitiless, it did.

Oddly, I forgot to raise the lid of the chest and look down into the bedroom below.

I washed in the cold standing water, combed my hair, and left it loose. My stockings I washed in the used liquid, and went out bare-legged in my shoes.

The stair wound round and round, like something in the stem of a church tower. I must have noticed this when I came up here, with the Grandmadame. Or else the stair had changed its nature. Reaching the bottom, I was dizzy and leaned on the wall.

There was the corridor, however, and so the gallery with the painting of the Dance of Death. In the daylight, this was crude and flaking, profound only because of its age. Unless, of course, it was a fake.

Below, over the gallery's wooden balustrade, lay the hall inside the front door of the house. It was large, and lit by a round window above the door. The white house-pillar that held up the roof was nothing of the sort. It was a kind of metal cylinder, painted or enamelled white. I deduced abstractedly that it was a Russian stove, something uncommon surely, here. In winter, it would be stocked with wood, and lighted, sending up its great heat through the house. There was a wooden floor.

Otherwise, save for the shields, swords, daggers and muskets on the walls, the hall was bare.

I glanced along the corridor to where, last night, the second lamp had burned, indicating the bedroom of Thérèse – and Julie. It was an ordinary cramped dark vista, and this one of those large dwellings bisected everywhere by narrow winding corridors that could not be walked with arms outstretched, crumpled and craning stairs, large bleak rooms. There would be mice, rats, wood-worm, decay, the miasma of a thousand births and deaths and the short angry interludes of lives.

When I got down, I descended into the lower house, and to the kitchen, and there I found the table used and abandoned. It was now one hour after sunrise. They had been and gone.

On the scrubbed surface, they had left – or had been left – half another of the dark loaves, this one once round, now a half moon, on a cracked white plate, the pitcher of water and a crooked greenish glass, a knife, and a single fruit, a pear, a perfect pear, glossy, the colour of pale polished wood with a pink-green blush. Who had put it there? Was it for me? And – how on earth – here in this primitive early summer-spring, had a pear been grown?

I crossed to the table – the arrangement was like a still life, spot-lit by the windows – and took the pear. I rubbed it on my jacket, and sank my teeth into it. The flesh was crystalline and white, and its juice flooded my mouth. I ate it cruelly and completely to the core. Then I drank the water.

To one side of the kitchen was a door I hadn't seen, which, therefore, had not existed the previous evening. I opened it with ease, passed down another corridor, where plants stood on window-sills, geraniums with trailing leaves, and spiders spun grey sugar on the panes, which were cracked. The second door was low, I must bow my head. I came out in a courtyard, cobbled, with a leaning stable-building to one side. The doves were busy here, flying to the house roofs and to a large dove-cote. An opening in the wall showed me fields and olive trees, and, far beyond those, again the forest, and the mountains.

Outside the wall, I walked down a parched track, and the wood pressed close on one side, and on the right, I saw into fields, the soil in black strips, and then the corn beginning, low, in yellowish stubble. Now I feel Anna at my shoulder. She tells me this could not be so. Not the corn, for this isn't the south, not yellow any way, and not so high so soon. Well, Anna, now there is a field where the corn is high to my knees, because I wade out into it, yellowish-green I admit, and there are scarlet poppies growing.

I heard her singing, Julie's child, and saw her abruptly, straight through the stalks, bending in her faded frock, to pick the poppies.

"Don't," I said.

She looked up, stopped her song. She seemed neither disturbed nor annoyed, yet I said, "That's what she did, Persephone. She pulled up a red poppy and the earth opened. The god of death came and seized her, carried her off. Then her mother had to go looking for her, all over the world, poor Demeter."

"It was because she was so beautiful," said the weird-looking child. "That is why the god took her."

I said, firmly, unkindly, "It was because she pulled up the poppy."

"Why?"

"If you pull up the poppy, you kill it. If you kill anything, you attract him, King Death."

I didn't know why I had spoken to her. Children bore and tax me. But... she was Julie's, child? Julie must have borne her.

I thought of the contradiction. Isis seeking Osiris, who eventually became god of the dead. And Demeter seeking Persephone, seized by the god of death. I had already written in my mind the phonetic Egyptian spelling of Osiris, *Ousir*. Its comparison to the name d'Ouest had not been lost.

The child bent and pulled another of the flowers. It was the colour of fire, with a black eye.

As I came up to her, she lifted the poppies and let me smell them. They had the scent of earth.

She looked very feral, this child, with her harsh bare feet. Her face was brown, her eyes certainly yellow as a hawk's.

We walked on side by side, and the corn reached to my knees and just beneath her bosom. She had one, actually. She was already not only a child. Did she bleed too, poppy red?

"Who is Maman?" I asked.

She thought. She said, "Madame Thérèse."

"And your father – Papa..."

She didn't answer.

Then the olive trees came back. They were silvery. I don't know, Anna, should they have been?

We sat down, among the talons of their roots. The child began to weave a poppy crown. She sang again. She seemed not to mind me. I tilted back my head and looked through the feathers of the olives at the pale blue sky.

How many times had men fucked me? Again and again. Yet I had never conceived. Was I barren? If not, one day, I might have a child.

Slyly, surreptitiously, I gazed sidelong at this one. What would I do with her, my child? Would I tell her stories? Had my mother told me stories? Did I know how?

I had slept during the night and there had been dreams, but I could recall none of them, although now I thought one dream concerned my mother. I couldn't decipher it.

Instead I recollected later, when I had been in the hotel room in Paris, and Julie had had me, before her, I had been with a sailor on the boat. His semen had been inside me, and I had not had the chance or energy or fastidiousness to wash it away. Had

I smelled of him? The heat of shame rose from my womb, and in that moment, the child raised her head, left her song, and announced, "There is Papa!" I think she spoke in French.

Through the corn I saw the rider coming up, from the direction of the mountains, towards the house. The horse was white, freckled, like milk glass. Its mane and tail were coal black.

On its back, Julie.

A gentleman's clothes, dark, spare, for the country and for riding. The boots were worn, the silky waistcoat, the coarse shirt. Hatless, and the raven hair, a wing fluttering, longer than I remembered, to the top of the shoulder-blades. The face so clear, in daylight now, and total vision, with its high colour and arched black brows, and the black eyes and chiselled lips and long straight nose. The face of a young man, so it was, a man of delicacy and genius, of brooding stature and quicksilver temper. Arrogant and cool. But also hot, also unsure, hesitating. A sword, a caress, a momentary elegant stammer that would break the heart.

I stood up, but all through me, melted, made weak, I could not run or even walk. I stumbled forward, and she-and-he was gone. And I heard the little sound, the little instruction, and the hoofs of the horse pick up. And as I surged and burst from the grain, they had galloped away. I might have shouted. My voice would crack. She would not hear. I was dumb. I could not speak or swallow, and suddenly leaning over myself, I gave a kind of groan, like the noise of pleasure. Is it possible to die of such a thing? Oh, yes. But I didn't. I hadn't the sense to. Not then.

The child laughed, and I turned, my eyes blurred and my body swinging to and fro, to see if she jeered at me.

But she was playing some private game, with the poppies.

"Your *father*?" I asked.

She looked up. "Yes."

"Will you run after him?"

"No. I won't see him until tonight. Perhaps not until tomorrow."

"Why not?"

Again, she did not bother to answer. It was patently so obvious, the mysterious and obscure reason.

And I, with slow dragging steps, went up through the fields, bare now, with just the whiskers of corn showing, following the white horse and the dark rider, seeing the hoof prints in the soil.

But when I regained the house, and the yard, no one was there. The stable was empty as before. The doves flew about, presumably troubled by my psychic, silent cries.

There was no one in that house. Not through the long and sultry day, which, with the afternoon, grew stormy, the sky charcoal blue and massed with architectural clouds. And yet, they must have been there. Somewhere.

What did I do? I went from room to room and all about the stairs and corridors. I opened cupboards and found things, piles of sheets edged with embroidery, mean broken yellow candles, a tinderbox, the ghastly bald head of a doll with only one eye. There was a chest, too, on a landing, locked up tight. It was carved with figures. It smelled like the incense from a church. Perhaps a body was packed in it. I sensed the dead everywhere, not the living. There were a lot of chairs.

In the afternoon, as the storm came, I was empty and went down and found the half loaf and ate a piece. The bread was full of uncooked grain and grit. But a brown bottle had appeared on the table, and in it was a fiery spirit, brandy maybe, with which I sluiced the mouthfuls down.

During the storm, which must have started about three o'clock, from the position of the sun, I returned to my attic. I lifted the lid of the chest with the spy hole, and looked through.

Did I anticipate seeing her, lying there on that bed, in the arms of her wife?

The bed was made, the quilts pulled up, and the feather pillows, with their edgings of lace, piled deep. In the middle of it all lay the dog, on his back. He snored.

I had only to wait. The child had told me. Tonight. Tomorrow.

Desperately then I wanted to bathe. Why? Did I expect – anything? Of course, I could expect nothing. It was the heat. The prickly, itchy quality of the stormy air. But no bathrooms had been found in this ancient corrupt house, at least not by me.

I washed again, every inch of me, in the small quantity of scummy water in the basin, making the towel very wet, but in a few hours more it was dry as a bone.

I lay down on the bed I had been given, naked. I stretched out my arms sideways, and my legs were a little apart. Irresistibly, I imagined that she would pass in at the door. I thought of her narrow long hands on me. In half sleep, a slow throbbing tide of pleasure, aching as a tooth, swelled in the opening of my sex, heavier and more urgent, until at last I brought my thighs together as Agnes had done, and squeezed orgasm into and out of myself.

The thunder boomed against the house and the window darkened.

When I woke, the sky was light again, although with the cast of later afternoon. Beyond the pane, when I looked, the sunny olive trees and the forest – even the lime avenue – were spangled, and the wild lawn, with the rain that must have fallen. Directly below, the girl in the green basin concealed her bosom and her groin, but the silver sweat was also on her – what had she been doing to herself?

I dressed in my skirt and the clean and crumpled blouse from my bag.

Into the oval mirror I looked.

Ah, yes, now, still it is the face of desire. A hungry face. Do I recognise you, Esther? Have I ever? And, in future, shall I look at you and think, in fear, but who is *this?*

Downstairs, the birdsong had grown thick as weaving. All through the stone walls of the house it entered, like the light, which now showed things off and did not hide them. And there was the aroma of rich cooking.

But this was the house of the Beast in the tale of Beauty. Invisible servants put things ready – water and soap – the bread, a perfect pear, a bottle of spirit – and now did they cook food for me? Who was then the *Beast?* Julie? Or a composite of them all: Grandmother, wife, child and dog.

Henri was on the steps to the kitchen, he barked at me and ran up, flapping his tail. I bent and touched his head. After all, I thought he saved my life when the other one – the one Grandmadame had indeed called a beast, the red-head who was a man – had tried to burn me alive. Or pretended to.

The kitchen was a hot jewel of flame. The lambent afternoon, and the lamplight too. And the hearth was awake, burning up, dancing.

Before the table stood a girl, a child-girl, with brown hair. Her face was flushed. From a bowl she spooned a spicy mustard – I could smell it easily – on to a leg of meat, pork, in a black tin where fat bubbled.

She raised her head. It was the one who was 'Julot's wife'. The named one, Thérèse.

She did not seem to know or not know me. *She* seemed familiar, in the way strangers are. We are used to strangers.

But she smiled.

She said, in hesitant but exact English, "Good afternoon, m'mselle."

"I thought I was called a number here," I said brazenly. "Thirty-Four."

And she laughed. A lovely liquid sound. She finished spooning the amber mustard on to the pork, slid the black lid upon the tin, and put the whole back on the black rungs over the fire. Then, the protective greasy cloth in her hands, she straightened again. She was like me. I could see it plainly, and could she?

Between us rested the table, crowded now, two purplish cabbages, a heap of withered, cider-scented apples, bunches of dark green herbs, onions made of copper.

"You are Esther," she said, "and I am Thérèse. It is the same name."

And she dipped the spoon from the dregs of the mustard, and wrote, in mustard, on the table-top, this:

Es Ther

Ther Es (e)

Tiny hairs rose on my scalp.

"That's strange."

"Why?" she said. She wiped her small hand on her apron, and held it out to me.

I had come round the table to the hot fire, to see the writing in hot mustard. I took her hand, meaning to shake it. Instead I raised it to my lips. I was famished. She was perfumed with mustard and roasting pork, cabbage, onion, rosemary. I could have bitten a piece out of her.

When I stepped back, the dog was in the kitchen, innocent and open-mouthed, and Thérèse tossed to him one of the alcoholic apples. Now I saw him eat quite daintily.

Moving away, I sat on the stool the child had used before.

"What do you know about me?" I said.

"Only a little."

There was silence, but for the dainty rending of Henri with the apple. Thérèse began to slice onions. She was immune to their strength, but my own eyes watered, and this was like the tears that had torn through my pupils, spying on her, with the child, and the story of Demeter, the notion of mothers.

After the onions, she sliced the apples and the cabbages. A great iron pan stood by with a pool of oil, and there she scattered some green herbs lavishly, and white-pink slivers of garlic.

"And your husband," I said, "*Julot*..."

She glanced at me. She was amused.

"You may call my husband *Julie,* to me."

I rubbed the onion tears from my eyes and said, in rage, "How can you be married to a woman?"

Thérèse shrugged. "I am. How not?"

"And what do you think of me?"

"You're very pretty."

I shook myself. I said, "And the child – is she yours – or *hers*"

"Hers and mine."

"Oh no. That really isn't credible."

"Are you so sure, then," said Thérèse, "about the laws of this world?" The apples were like dice, the cabbages were all in strips, the green of the forest leaves, veined purple as marble. They might be made of anything but cabbage. She looked at them and relented. "I won't tease you, Esther. Obviously, this is my daughter by Julie's brother."

"The one with the red hair who dressed as a woman."

Henri met the apple core and gave up his daintiness, he gobbled pith and pips, the life of the fruit.

"Where is she now, your husband?"

"She is here."

"And you cook this meal for her?"

"For us," said Thérèse.

"Why for me? I can't be welcome, can I? The intruder. Do

you know…"

"Oh, yes," she said. Again she looked at me.

"Number Thirty-Four," I said. "If that's really true. How sick of it all you must be."

"Why?" she repeated.

"If a *man* is married to a woman, he philanders – and she hates it." I said this, and ceased. I felt the former thing. That I was making something occur, forcing it, forcing myself to feel the *proper* emotions, and she too, this unknown known one, trying to force her, this Thérèse, whose name was a virtual anagram of mine, or mine of hers.

She said, "You see how silly that all is."

I said, "And do you know about the spy hole in the attic?"

"Oh... that – of course."

"And I've spied on you."

Thérèse, smiling: "And what did you see?"

"You – told the child a story of Demeter and Persephone. And the other child, in the fire."

She had finished her vegetables, and laid the knife aside. "Did you like this, my story?"

I blurted out, "I wanted to hear the end."

She said, "Then, I'll save it for you."

Henri had come creeping over the flagstones. He lurked before the hearth. His hackles rose and he snarled. He had identified the pork.

"And is it," I said, "that the dog is a pig?"

Thérèse crossed to a cupboard and drew out a tall stoppered bottle, this one of black vitreous. She returned and filled for me the greenish glass that had remained among the cabbages and onions on the table. The drink was colourless. I didn't know what it was. Poison? No, we had all dispensed with that.

"Let me, for now, tell you another story," said Thérèse, and she drank from the glass, and handed it to me. "In the village where you arrived after your train, there is a church. In the church is a statue of the Virgin."

"That's common enough," I said.

"But this Virgin is dressed very beautifully. She has a sky-blue veil that was brought from the East, and a dress of white muslin stitched with golden stars. Inside these fine soft clothes, the statue is made of bronze." Thérèse watched me drink. She said,

"When you go to her, they pull back for you the hem of her dress. And you see that she has one lovely bare foot, and one foot that is deformed. It's a shapeless lump. But there is a cause. It is because whoever wants to, kisses the foot. For her blessing. You know that the Virgin stands between humanity and God, she intercedes. And he will always listen. She became pregnant by God without any physical possession, as the glass is pierced – do you see? – by the ray of the sun."

I thought of Agnes, what she had said. Pleasure, joy, glory, without breaking the seal.

And, as if I couldn't help it, I thought of the gardener who broke into me, and how I made out I was glad, to save, it seemed to me, my life. Breakage without pleasure, joy or glory. Barren necessity.

"My meaning is this," said Thérèse, "that the statue is made of hard bronze, and both her feet, once flawless, also of bronze, but the kisses of the hundreds who love her have worn away one foot. I mean, do you see, Esther, that if kisses can reshape hard metal, what can't they do to flesh and the heart? Don't cry," said Thérèse.

"The onions," I said.

She handed me from her pocket a small square of clean linen edged with the lace of this house. Her sweet handkerchief. Just what my mother had done, when I was a child. But I hadn't even cried. That had been Anna.

Julie didn't join the party. I had known she wouldn't. I had stopped longing for it or dreading it. It was as if she were not there, or there only as the night, which descended mote by mote, beyond the ambience of our fires.

The grandmother came, Grandmadame, as I'd realised she must. But she wore a crimson dress, and her hair partly up and some hanging, and this reached her hips. In her ears were gold earrings, two drops, that, when you looked, were suns. The child wore a green dress and had also put up her hair, perhaps by herself, like a courtesan. Thérèse and I, who had been cooking, wore our work-a-day clothes and had red cheeks from the hearth. Henri sat on his stool, and a plate was put before him.

They explained, he would not eat the pork, but the fried cabbage, apple, onion, the potatoes boiled in their skins and in the drink from the black bottle, then fried in olive oil with rosemary, these Henri would accept.

There was red wine, rough, in chipped cheap glasses, tasting of stone – the wine, the glass, who knows.

We ate, laughing and drinking.

And the child had brought some of the nasty broken candles from the cupboards, and stuck them on saucers, and they blazed, every one a different height, a different shade of yellowishness, from honey to milk. The light – the light! It was quite beautiful. Like the heart of the moon. The centre of a brazier not hot enough to harm. And the scent of the burning, fragrant with myrrh, and the secret essence of a bee-hive, which is ruled by a queen.

My God, I remember it so well, that dinner in that kitchen, in the heart of that red moon.

But not – what was said. Not one word.

Only laughter, flavours, lights, faces.

And the face of the dog as relevant as our own.

What were we? The phases of the moon, maybe, red or white. The old woman the gibbous moon, the child, new moon, and Thérèse and I the nubile middle lunar aspect – one who had given birth and one who had not, one acting a wife, one who acted as a whore. Agnes should have been there too, nubile, lessoned, but virgin still.

Yet Henri, what was he, a male animal, cross of boar and hound, glutton and guard, clown and magician.

I did not even eventually think of Julie, who had no place in this, and was not present. Although we bloomed, we played, in the entity of Julie. Without her, we would not be together, nor so alive.

Then the candles burnt down, were low and very rich. The child was sleepy and leaned against her mother's shoulder. The dog snored, his nose and front paws on the table.

The old gibbous moon of the grandmother put something in front of me.

The words grow clear again. Now I hear them.

"Do you see this?"

"A toy."

"Clockwork," said Grandmadame.

It was a carriage, about the size of a cup, and it had six horses to draw it. The gilt and paint had worn away, yet the forms were fine, still.

Grandmadame turned a key in the side of the coach, and it made a rasping sound, certainly like a clock, thinking if it would go or not. And then the horses twitched their little feet, and the wheels turned, and off it set, across the table.

The child watched with comatose glowing eyes. The dog took no notice. Thérèse turned away. She rested her lips on her daughter's curls which, by magic, she was changing into gold.

"What do you think?" asked the Grandmadame. I had the preposterous notion she wanted to sell it to me, the clockwork coach and horses.

"How old is it?"

"Some years, a hundred years. More."

The coach and horses had reached the end of the table, and as though intelligently perceiving the drop, halted.

"It's clever."

"There are several things. They were collected, or made. Quite old. But they still work, you see, with a little attention."

She rose, and stretching out, took up one of the larger candles that was still burning strongly.

"Come with me. I'll show you a curiosity."

There was silence in the room that had been full of the sounds of our party.

The eyes of the child and of her mother, Thérèse, were closed. It seemed to me that now I had been turned away, by those closed lids. And I must go instead with the waning moon of the old lady, and that this was sinister and fraught with some peril.

I got up anyway. And Grandmadame looked into my face with her basalt eyes. She seemed fundamentally wicked. It was all there in her mask, like a fox or monkey, wicked in the way of something not human, that need have no conscience and so will never hesitate.

"I'm tired," I said.

"So you say. But this will intrigue you."

Thérèse, not glancing at us said, softly, "We'll take the other stair, of course."

"Of course you will," said the Grandmadame. She went towards the door and the steps that led up into the house.

I saw, as I followed her, the dog was squinting at me, frowning.

I thought, perhaps she would lead me outside, the bitch, and kill me in the dark, stick a dagger into me. When we were on the steps, the friendly dulled light of the kitchen fading behind us, I said, "What are you going to do?"

"Very little," she said. "But you. You want to see Julot, don't you?"

I had been somnolent, at an ebb, and even the prospect of murder hadn't really woken me up.

But at this name, this *wrong* name, everything fell from me. I was weightless, unrelaxed, had eaten nothing, drunk only enough to electrify my brain.

"Julie," I said.

"Julot."

"Julot, then. Where is – he?"

"Patience. First, the curiosity. That is part of it, as you will see."

We had reached the hall, where the white Russian stove stood gleaming in the dark. Over the door, the round of glass, quite blind. The candle she carried glinted on those weapons and shields on the walls. And on one new thing. Between the pillar of the stove and the door, a sort of chair — I took it for that. It had a long thin back, and a bar that stretched out straight across this back. The seat was also narrow, ending in four curved legs. There were some peculiar carvings on them, and on the bar, and on the spine – like leaves they seemed to be. The chair faced towards the gallery above, and turning to look that way, I saw the ghosts of the mural, the Mediaeval Death Dance, the figures flirty and moving to the pulse of the candle.

There was no other light. If any lingered below, in the kitchen, now it was obscured. If any stars were above the forest, they did not show in the window over the door.

The carvings on the chair seemed to be moving, too, in the trick of the fluctuating flame.

"Clockwork," said the Grandmadame.

"The chair?"

"That. A great curiosity, I can assure you."

I said, to humour her, "What does it do?"

"You will discover, perhaps."

She went forward, and stood over the chair, and so I followed her.

It was of old dark wood, and incredibly smooth, shimmering like something not even hard at all, spilled ink or molasses.

"Do you see?" she said. She lowered the light, and I saw the carvings on the curious cross-piece. They were two little pretty long-fingered hands carved out of wood, and the digits charmingly jointed. They rested near the chair's central upright, but at the other ends of the bar, were two crescents, coiled back. These I failed to understand. But, my eyes going after the progress of the candle, I saw now four other small hands, two perched higher, and two low down, on the spine of the chair. And then, lying on the seat, two more, equally exquisitely fashioned, with a delicacy worthy of the most adorable and elegant doll. But these two hands lay open as flowers, their palms spread and fingers slightly curled.

"Hands," I said. "A chair of hands."

She pointed to the front legs of the chair. A hand lay too on both of these. And at the bottom of each leg, another crescent, thrust off. I realised what the crescents were, both pairs. The cuffs of hinged manacles, lying stiff, undone and ready.

I felt nothing. Or is that true? The Grandmadame had always been a foe. Who isn't?

She said, "Do you think it will fit you?"

"I don't want to sit in it."

"How can it hurt you?"

"There are fastenings," I said, "to restrain."

"Quite right. So there are. Why is that, I wonder?"

I saw now that a sort of rod extended from the base of the chair along the floor, and then she put her foot on this and at that the chair quivered. All the pairs of fairy hands fluttered like the wings of small birds, and the fingers made infinitesimal, almost *beckoning*, signs.

"Are you not fascinated?" she said.

"No."

"Suppose," she said, "I tell you Julot – *Julie* – will come on to the gallery. Will stand on the gallery, there, and look at you. But only if you sit in this chair."

My mouth was dry and I was trembling. But I did not properly know why. I thought I should run by her, and if Julie was in the house now, I should call out to her. It was simple. One did not require this silly, possibly dangerous, game.

"You have no idea," she said to me. "Can you be such a fool? I tell you. If you sit in the chair, *She* will come."

"Your son."

"She, my son"

My legs had no bones in them. I was heavy, at once warm and cold. There was nowhere to fly to but the forest and the boar with his bristled bottle of a snout.

"All right. Very well."

"Not so fast. First you must take off your clothes. Ah, no. Not for me. I have no interest that way. But for Julie. Julie will like it. And otherwise, you can hardly experience the *cleverness* of this chair. Naked. Everything. Hurry now."

She was like a school mistress. She had the precise tone of Miss Much. The shadow across her hand might be a cane.

I knew now, obviously. I was scornful. I was impervious. As for my body, everyone had seen it. I had nothing to hide physically.

I undid my clothes and threw them down, and turned and stood before her. Her face did not change. It was a fact, she was indifferent, or primed only to other things. "Sit."

I lowered myself on to the narrow seat, which supported me, yet very firmly and slightly raised between my legs.

"Your arms up," she said, "along the bar."

So I raised my arms, a crucifixion pose, and, placed on the bar, so very smooth, like the seat, my wrists were where the manacles would come down. Then she pointed to my feet, I must shift them farther apart, and there my ankles were, against the chair legs, ready for the other manacles. I was, too, held open, and my breasts lifted, offered. If I hadn't known, I must have, at this point.

"I shall shut you in," she said, matter-of-factly. "Are you afraid?"

"You are so wonderfully *kind*, you and your royally gracious family," I said, "why should I be?"

She grunted shortly. She said, "When I have fastened the stays, I shall start the clockwork. It will last a few minutes.

120

During this time, Julie will appear, up there."

It was easy to see, up over the partition, where the Dance of Death went on, skipping and gambolling.

"And then," said the Grandmadame, "it is between you and she."

At those words, a bolt of panic – or of blackest lust – passed through me. Which? And against the wood of the narrow crafty seat I surged, engorged. If I had been male, she could have laughed at me.

But now she only looked withered and elderly, stupid, slow. She put out her hands and snapped down the restraints over my wrists. They were firm but not uncomfortable. Bending – and I heard her corset or her bones creak – she did the same to the clasps at my ankles. Was I powerless? Yes, so it would seem. Physically so. But the body itself enslaves, enchains. This wasn't really new.

She stepped back a pace. She was the curator, I the waxwork. She was bored with me, had seen me so often. She plunged her foot down upon the rod in the floor. And like the toy coach and horses – a very model of the vehicle that had almost run me over in Paris – the chair rasped and coughed and I felt it come to life as if blood were flowing through its veins.

I was to ignore the chair of torture or pleasure. I would stare up at the gallery. Waiting. It was dark without the candles.

It did not occur to me Thérèse or the child would enter the hall. I knew they wouldn't. These bizarre events were for a stage Thérèse did not, probably, ascend. The dog might come. That might be funny.

But I was alone.

The chair vibrated. At first, only that. But then naturally, the pretty delicate hands slipped on to my cool flesh, there in the dark. They were animate, restless. Yet you could mistake them for nothing live.

The pair on the cross-bar began. They negotiated daintily into the tender hollows on my inner arms, and stroked me, up and down, circling a little, and to the vulnerable area of my wrists, and back. They seemed to seek to reassure me, intimately of course, like a hand slipped in under an arm, inside the crook of the elbow. Naughty little hands. After these, the next pair crept up across my breasts. These were bolder now. They palmed me, slid over me, testing me, and at the buds of my nipples, a terrible sightless seeking, they fingered over and over, trying me, asking me to give them in return an answer. My nipples hardened. How could they not? The third pair alighted on my ribs. They caressed me, to my waist, and down over my belly, and up again. You could tell, they liked the feel of me. They told me so. They savoured me. Over and over, and over.

I had shut my eyes. I could hear my breathing. My head fell back.

On my calves, behind my knees, making me twitch in a tiny spasm, two other waking hands. At their urging, helpless, my legs relaxed. I sprawled, and the seat of the chair began to shift against me. Now these two ultimate hands, which had been the clue, stealthy, slinking, seemed to have been trained to their work. It was no longer feasible to believe they could not think. They were not human, not animal. Yet they were – creatures.

The forward hand swam to my loins and shiveringly fixed on to the purse of flesh, parted, sought, came to touch, to tremble, with a feathering thumb – how had such dexterity been fashioned? – the nub of me, nub against nub. While the long finger coaxed itself on and into me, as if into a glove. These too, this finger, this thumb, asked their question. Especially the finger was asking, yes, and the thumb prompted. And the finger – it asked, it asked. It must have an answer. Wouldn't I – wouldn't I...?

The hand at the base of my spine, that fondled, as if it knew me after all, and knew what I would say. But the finger of this hand, curious, had reached the anal mouth, and did not quite dare. It began and went on, circling round me, playing over me. Shall I? No, no. I mustn't. But I must, I *must*. I'll just play here, like a leaf moving to the fall of a recurring rain-drop. But, I'd like to. Oh, let me. It's nothing... is it? Oh, let me. Yes. No? No, yes.

I could not make a sound. I had stoppered myself up. But my breathing, and the faint noise of the chair, and some rhythm of my own, arching myself, my spine tautening as my legs and arms dissolved.

Trying to keep my eyes on the gallery, but all in the dark now. No one – no one anywhere.

I refused to give in to it. Yes, it had me helpless. But the climax, the *crise*. Not that. Think of the filthy drunken man in the rented room, his old hat on the table, his dirty hands with green nails – my teacher at the college. Think of the raping gardener, ready to kill if I would not, since I had provoked him by being alive and female.

But oh, I must, oh, let me, says the chair. You see, I'm only wood, only sweet small wooden fingers. How lovely this is. Nothing pressed on you. Nothing to breathe in your face. How lovely, lovely. Say how it is. Is it lovely?

And Miss Much, who shut me into the lavatory. I was sick. Vomiting frightens me, sneezing, letting go. And this is much more. I won't.

But let me. Ah, touch you, yes. Nipples and breasts, arms and knees, ankles, wrists. And the waist, and the belly. And here inside, vulva, vagina, anus. Oh, these silver ripples of deliciousness, ah this warm entrance – is it opening – just a little – oh, let me, let me. Only the fingers of dear little dolls. Only a chair. A chair that kisses. *Baisser* – fucks…

I make a sound. My eyes fly wide.

There on the gallery – Death comes to life, perhaps. A young man, black hair, slender. No, it is Julie.

See what you've brought me to.

She stands upright. She watches me. A hint of light from somewhere that shows just the edges of her face, and on her hair, her hand on the gallery panel. A hand.

But these hands aren't hers. No need to resist.

I struggle. Towards her? Away? To leave the chair? To dance on the chair. My mother danced. Look where it got her. All I can remember – her face without features, lights on the edges…

I won't let you go until you come. So some old man said. And I made believe. Naturally. I had heard that woman in the hotel. And Mr Golden with his penis in Mrs cross-eyed Miriam's mouth.

But Julie made me. And Agnes made me. And I have made myself. A lesson learned.

Julie steps back, and she's gone. She doesn't want to see after all.

And the chair of hands... slackening. It too grunts. It doesn't care anymore. The clockwork is running down.

I'm lying stranded, washed up. An ache like a scorched, hard black plum presses at the base of my stomach. I shudder. Cold, hot. Ice and fires.

Julie comes out from the door that leads to the gallery stair. I can see her clearly, though there is no light. She comes up to me, is standing over me.

How beautiful she is, whatever she is, man or woman, both.

"You want more?" she asks me. As she did in Paris.

"No. Let me out. Disgusting – this is disgusting."

I think that the house door may burst open, and the boar canter in, with the red-headed brother leading him.

She says, Julie, "You followed me. Didn't you want to find me?"

"Let me out," I say, quite calmly.

She says, "But I like it. I like to be watching it. Don't you like me to see? If it was myself, as you are – what then?"

And I think of her, think of her as she is, not naked, as I am, but manacled in this chair. And her head thrown back, arching, clenched and insane with orgasm – and as I think of it, she, like Grandmadame, steps hard on the rod, and everything begins again, without preliminary now, and as it does so, all the flickering and fingering and stroking and lisping and pleading, she leans over me, and I can smell her scent of skin and hair.

The pain in my womb and colon melts, becomes marvellous. A spasm comes in, a wave on to my shore. I am flung over, into death. I know now what it is. Annihilation.

The waves of agony that are delight pass through me, and through and through me. It won't end. Like Agnes. I can do nothing. I am hung upside down from the moon of the dead.

Life – life is the Dance of Death.

Whoever dances must die.

I've forgotten her, forgotten them all. Nothing. Adrift. Into the Western Lands, under the world. Down and down.

The hall is built of my screams. I can still hear them, though they were over an hour ago.

She hasn't touched me. Who is she? I forget.

And *she*, lying in this chair, so comfortless, too narrow, its mechanism stopped: Who is *this* she, lying here?

"Let me out," she says again. I lift my head up, and through her tears, I say, "Let me out."

But then I find the manacles are undone.

Julie assists me to get up and wraps some garment around

me, perhaps even a melodramatic cloak. I can't walk and she supports me, half carries me. I cry. I can hear myself crying. Everything is lost. But I never had a thing, anyway.

Just before we left the Egyptian city, after the scandal broke concerning our father and Mr Golden and some business venture, something disreputable, Anna and I went into the garden of the mansion we could see in the rue Des Palmes, the pillared mansion with the lemon blossom.

I think it was a garden party. There were coloured parasols, and I recall an enormous cake, on which the flies were always busily settling, but servants whisked them away, smiling to reassure us all, as they prayed we would contract typhoid or dysentery.

Anna and I, eleven, twelve, something like that, moving through the haze of an Egyptian afternoon. I thought the garden was like the Garden of Eden, and wished it emptied of people. I searched for the Apple Tree, but there were so many trees, all flowering in my memory, as surely they couldn't have all been, and the perfumes of orange and jacaranda and lemon and lilac, and the toffee smells of our own washed bodies, and the musk on the skins of women, and cigarettes, and spoiling elaborate food.

We wore gloves and white hats. Otherwise we might have been naked, for all I can recall of our clothes. Appropriate, of course, if it had been the Garden of Eden.

In the end, the garden *was* emptied. Rain poured from the sky – ah, so then I do remember rain there, after all. That once.

My father, already under suspicion, not shunned but treated with care, as if too hot to touch, stood on a long veranda, and watched the rain. But I stood on the lawn, which was dry and brown. I stood in the rain.

It was obvious to me then, even then, that not much is real, and yet, the unreality is, if anything, more pressing, more convincing than truth. I was soaked, the food was soaked, puddling off the table in white and pink sloshes, runnelling down the flower beds, and frogs jumped by with blancmange on their backs. And all this because of the unreal rain. No one had expected it. It happened to cause harm.

I saw my father, and beheld he was a thing with two arms, two legs, a head, a body. And I saw how alien this arrangement was, as if I had come from some other world, and was another organism entirely.

Anna called me over and over. She would not come into the unreal soaking rain for fear of the wet. Finally, one of the servants brought me into the house, into the long white room of fans and ferns and lattices. They thought I was upset, because of the scandal, although I'd been told nothing. I had stood in the rain from distress, confusion, so I heard them muttering. But I stood in the rain because it wasn't real. Even if it had drowned me.

We were in the corridor, in blackness. She held me close to her. I felt the beating of her heart. She had a woman's breasts, shallow, firm. She kissed my neck, my shoulder. She kissed me without desire, but faithfully. Kisses that wear away the shape of metal.

I said her name. "Julie."

It must never stop, this moment. To be held, to be kissed like this. In darkness. With her.

But at last she let me go, and now I could stand perfectly well.

"Tomorrow," she said, "you should leave. There will be money, everything you need. A man will take you to the station. His cart is clean and he will be quite respectful to you."

"No," I said. But I knew this denial was meaningless.

She was only a foot or so away from me. Yet I could no longer reach her. I sensed her faint warmth. I wanted to lie against her body, but I had done that. It was over.

"Well," I said, "now Thirty-Four is finished with. Punished and shamed and her sex burnt out of her, and comforted and sent packing. And then, there will be Thirty-Five. In the summer, perhaps. But she may be circumspect, she may not pursue you here. She may not even like you."

"I agree that may be the case."

I said, "Won't you let me – can't I…?" I wanted to ask her to let me sleep in a bed with her. Not to seek for any act of arousal

– the machine had riven all that from me, and it seemed I should be sterile of desire for ever – as was supposed to happen, if one saw snakes copulating. As, until she touched me, I had been. But I couldn't say it anyway, for I knew she wouldn't lie down with me. What had she had from me, what had she done to me? The chair, with its awful and obscene enforcement of pleasure. As if to demonstrate that another person, even she, was not necessary, not at all. Only a mechanism, which anyone might have started. Probably which one could, with practice, start oneself.

"Go and sleep now," she said. "Look, there's the door."

She took my hand and put it over a latch. Let my hand fall.

The unreal rain of her absence, of her going from me, of my going from her, and never again, never again – into the unreal rain I went, opening the door, soaked to the soul, and drowning.

And found myself in the pearl-lit bedroom with the pillows edged by lace. And in the bed, lying looking at me with her quiet eyes, Thérèse.

She persuaded me to get into bed beside her, and I don't recall how this was done. Did I think now I was to be meat for her? Or she, for me... No, I think I was numb and dazed and didn't prevaricate, I simply dropped my covering and climbed into the high old bed. And Thérèse, in her nightgown, put her arm about me.

I lay against her, and she gave me sips of chocolate from a blue cup. She told me the ending of the story of Demeter and Persephone, which I had always known. I floated towards sleep in her arm, and some of the story was a dream. How Demeter learned at last her child was in the cold hell of the dead, wife to the King of Death. Demeter was granted the ability to reclaim her only if Persephone had eaten nothing in the Underworld. Of course, she had. Seven pomegranate seeds. And what are they, then, but the semen of a god? She had made love with Death, loved him so well that she had swallowed his seed. And so, Demeter might have her back for only half the year, or one third, in certain versions. And for the other half or the other two thirds, Persephone stayed with her lover underground.

In the end, asleep, I dreamed I was with Julie again. We were on a hill above the corn fields, and the corn was high and the wind blew it in waves, a saffron sea.

I felt only happy. The overpowering emotions had gone from me, sexual and emotional lust, jealousy, rage and hurt. Instead there were other emotions, quite new, bright as minted gold. How can I describe them? We don't feel such things. Perhaps... wild joy without hysteria, nostalgia without regret.

We talked in the dream. I don't remember the words. I knew that I was dead, and in another country. And everything was well.

In the morning, the bed was empty but for me. The house, when I went down into it, again, empty, but I thought I heard Henri barking merrily in the fields of the Golden Land of the West.

The man waited with the cart on the drive. He was quite respectful, though he had no English, and indicated things by gesture. The cart was clean.

We travelled through the green forest. I tried to note it carefully, that bird on a bough, that rock beside that stream, but everything dispersed. Shadows.

At the station, he gave me a packet which contained a ticket, even a place in the dining-car for every meal, a berth to sleep in. There was money besides, lots of it.

When he had gone, the porter came up the platform in his red scarf. And one chicken, golden-brown as an egg, ran for cover into the lane.

Then the train must have arrived. But I remember nothing of it. I remember nothing of the journey. Perhaps I ate, or used the sleeping berth. Or did I stand in the corridor, watching the night and the fiery sparks blow by? I think I might have done.

In Pompeii there is an inscription on a tomb, *Here I am today, but where, tomorrow?*

You could say, too, *there* I will be tomorrow. But where am I, today?

I'd come to Paris for reasons I hadn't properly grasped, to

escape, to elude the responsibilities that we are told we must
adhere to. And when I got back to the city, I stood on the street
– my first next coherent recollection – and watched the pigeons
flying about in the sunlight. Paris, still grey, but pastel now, and
her flags flying. Paris with her architectures like crochet and her
river of mercury. Metal that moves.

Because I had some money, I picked along the boulevards,
staring at the cafes, like a destitute. Eventually I sat down at a
table and drank some coffee.

I had been there five minutes when a young man came up to
me. He was handsome and well-dressed, he spoke in French,
then, when I didn't reply, in halting English he asked if I would
lunch with him.

I said, "I'm so sorry, monsieur. But I have to go to the funeral
of my aunt."

"*Vôtre tante*," he said, gravely. "I am also so sorry. But later,
perhaps…"

"Ah, no, monsieur. I loved her."

When he had gone, I sat and reasoned how I still knew the
way to the bar in the rue Sac, the bar of the lobsters, where Agnes
worked.

She had told me head on that if we might not have Julie, we
might still have each other. It seemed to me that my sexual part
was destroyed, but even so, I could partake of her sweetness. Or
wouldn't she any more care for me? I knew that she would. I
knew that she would welcome me. Make some excuse to leave
her post. Fly home with me. Kiss me. Congratulate her toys on
my advent. Dress us both extravagantly, and then prepare some
wild faun's meal with garlic and herbs and eggs and wine.

If I couldn't yet love her, she would be patient.

With a searing poignancy, I thought of her loveliness. If I
couldn't love her, I was damned. She would forgive me. And
perhaps – perhaps – *later*, as my suitor had said, after the funeral
was over of my obsessive hopes... Later, perhaps.

As I reached the rue Sac, the sun was slanting over, reddish,
bronzish, and there were colours, the colours of sweets in paper.

But then I came to the bar. The opal tank of lobsters was
gone. The bar was closed, and across the door had been
hammered a board.

How long had I been gone – a handful of days.

I turned around, and around, bemused. And all the illusions of the street were there, but abruptly one became quite real. From the door of the *tabac* marched a little girl, about seven, and she rolled before her, into the victory of the light, a dog on wheels. I had seen it last in Agnes' room. The same one, without doubt, even to the patch on its side.

I ran across and stopped, and the child, oblivious of the antics of elders, paid no attention.

"Where did you get the dog?"

As I said this, it came to me I could not find the way to Agnes' room. There had been so many twists and turns. I had not concentrated. In any case, everything would be altered, to deceive me, as very often the streets of cities change themselves just for this purpose.

I said again: "The *dog*."

She looked up, the child, surprised. Why was this girl shouting at her in a foreign tongue?

I said, "*Le chien.*" Nothing else would come.

She smiled. She said gladly, "*Mon chien. Mon chien.*"

There was a woman in the doorway of the *tabac* now, and she called to me suspiciously, "*Vous êtes une Anglaise, oui?*"

"I'm sorry – *excusez-moi, madame* – but the dog – Agnes had the dog…"

"Ah." The woman crossed her arms. She looked long at me. She said, in English, "A friend to Agnes?"

"A very good friend – I came to – visit her – but the bar…"

"My English is little," she said, "walk in."

Inside the shop, the church smell of tobacco and scented snuff. An old man sat in a chair in the corner, with a rug on his knees, the red sun on his face through the doorway.

She muttered to him rapidly in French, and he turned to me. He spoke in English, heavily accented.

"Agnes… is your friend?"

"Yes – yes…"

"Madame brings you a cognac."

And then he got up, half crippled as he seemed to be, and led me to the seat, and put me down in it.

"Agnes comes in, and she has boxes on a cart. She says to Madame, you take my flowers, and the toys for the children. You understand," he says, "my son fathers fourteen children. And the young ones run up and they have all the toys. This makes them very happy. We afford only little. And the toys are very fine. But Madame says, are you leaving here? And Agnes says, Yes, I am leaving. And I see her, she is looking sad. Not anything else. But sad. So then she goes over to the bar."

Nothing more happens, only the children playing with the toys, and Madame arranging the new geraniums on window-sills, and finding in the boxes other things, scarves and beads, and she says to the old man, her father- in-law, this is strange, but she will talk to her husband when he comes back from the factory. Maybe Agnes has found a rich protector and is tired of her former possessions.

In the evening, about nine, there is a commotion in the bar. Now and then this occurs. In the end, however, the commotion is out on the street.

Madame stands in the doorway of the *tabac*, and tells the old man precisely what goes on. She never falters, he says, proudly, she is as good as a book for such things, even when she is sobbing in the end, just before she rushes across.

It seems there's a customer, a man who is drunk. He wants a lobster from the tank for his dinner. They tell him, in the bar, that there's a problem with the lobsters. They can't serve him. But then the man loses his temper. He begins to rave. He says it is always like this. Anything he wants he can't have. His wife won't sleep with him. His son hates him. His employer intends to sack him. And there is a woman he fancies, who has emptied stale water from a vase of roses over his crotch. And now, this. This business with the lobsters. So he comes out into the street, with a bottle of absinthe, to smash the lobster tank. The waiters pelt before him, trying to stop it, either because it is a scheme they have which makes them money, or they are fond of the lobsters, which have been there years. But he hurls the waiters away. He knocks them down. Then Agnes comes out and speaks to him. He turns to her, and there she is, curved and lovesome and golden. It's more than he can bear. He crashes the bottle straight down on her golden head. As she falls, he races off, part played, howling.

"She is dead at once," said the old man. "Not a mark, but for the blood running from her head. Her skull, they say, like an eggshell."

Madame was waiting by the counter and now she brought the brandy, mildly tipped up my chin, and poured it into me.

It sprang into my brain before the horror reached there. And so, as the horror entered with its banners of lightning, and after these, the train of empty loss, which mourns for those things we have never had, the brandy stood over me, and helped me to my feet, enabled me to speak politely, and led me back into the desert of the world.

CHAPTER FOUR

And So

Last night – or morning – I fell asleep in the way most people do, easily and naturally, about four a.m. Now and then, though not often, this happens. Perhaps it happens once every three months. But then, I woke at six, and my eyes were full of the cascading jagged scream of lights – the migraine. I was blind. And in the dark, I saw too much. I lay there, unable not to watch the lights that nothing could shut out, and the radio told me of a new illness that is destroying hundreds of people.

At seven, when the attack was over, I dozed, but woke after a few minutes, with what is called a 'hot flush'. The menopause sponsors these all night long. If asleep, it is like waking in a bath of almost boiling water, or on a bed of flame.

I didn't sleep anymore. They start getting up then. Water runs, lavatories flush, doors bang, radios, children. I lay and thought of pomegranates. I wanted one, and perhaps, if I went to the local supermarket, could buy one. Probably, if there weren't another migraine attack in the next two hours, it would hold off until tonight or tomorrow.

What did it mean, this fruit? I had read, the pomegranate is the womb, filled with bloody seeds, the ova of life. And if Persephone ate them, what did she eat? She was the fruit of Demeter, her mother's womb. Therefore *herself*? And for *that* reason then, did she stay with King Death?

I got up about eleven. I was exhausted. I always am. A shaft of light, a bar of shadow, these make me think I am about to go blind again. All the hours of wakefulness, these little shocks.

However, in the end, I went out, and found the pomegranate

after all in the corner shop, with three red apples.

The seeds are like stained glass, and the half apple like the pelvis of a woman. Of course, I can't eat pomegranate seeds – my teeth. But I eat them, while I can see, with my eyes.

In the rest of the house they make their usual noise. Hoovers, TVs, music centres, tapes. Or arguing. They don't go out much. No work. They get up every day from old habit.

There is no Anna to summon me to lunch. There is no Anna. You guessed. Anna is myself, my other half. Not of the apple. Not better.

And the father figure? Long gone.

I have one room, and outside, in the corridor, I share a bathroom with ten others. In my room is a low sink. I pee into it, then flush it with TCP and hot water. Constipation is a great boon.

All day the light is drinkable, like thin tea, then like wine. Finally comes the night, with her train of stars.

From my window by day no trees are visible, I can only see streets, and a view of a Victorian gasometer, a beautiful pale drum. But in the dark, a thousand lights evolve. Stars upon stars.

If there had been an Anna, earlier she would have slipped into my room, which would have been part of our house, with our father upstairs. She would have looked at the rest of my manuscript, asked if she could read it. I would have consented. Maybe in the evening, over our dinner, which she, the slave, had cooked, she would pick at the pages, saying this was wrong, and that, questioning, telling me, No, we never have been in Egypt, and Paris was not as I had said.

Well, I have been there. Just as I have written it. Egypt, and Paris. And then the house in the forest, Julie's house.

When I think of it now, the divine terror of the chair, which seemed to say I had only pursued the agony of sexual pleasure to the forest, and the moments after in the corridor, when she held me, my lover, as if I had pursued true love. My heart beats in heavy ponderous strokes. Julie is a phantom now. For, if I try to think of her, I know she must be old, or perhaps no longer alive. The story I've told, obviously, happened long ago. There have been wars since then, and how many battles of the flesh and heart.

How awful it was, telling all this. An electric pain. And how wonderful. Remembering how I was sent away from her, never having known her at all, and arriving in the city, sought Agnes again, who *was* true love perhaps. And for ever after, brandy would have the taste of graveyards. For the child had been dragged into the ground by Death.

Anna would say, "Oh, Esther. You live in your own head. That's where you go to. The places in *there.*"

But Anna won't say it. And upstairs there is no ninety-year-old man, upright as an iron poker, only a family with seven children who play video games late into the night, until twelve or one, when all the world, it seems, but for me, goes to sleep.

Oh, yes. Yes, Anna, every word is true. Because if I could see it, Anna, and if I felt it, Anna, it's as real as day or darkness. As real as the falling rain.

And I loved her, my Julie. Thank God, she can't see what I've become, that girl she held in her arms. Or did she? Did she? Of course she did, inside my skull, which the bottles of life haven't yet fractured.

Tonight, I don't sleep at all, not a moment, but as the radio cries on and on, I make a plan. I get up at 6 and wash my face in cold water. I eat some bread and Marmite for the serpent crawling in my belly. I am so fat now, I bang into things – I feel I hurt the furniture.

Anna would say I'm not careful. She would tell me furniture doesn't feel.

But Anna... Anna is me.

In the first light I go up, limping on my ruined feet and sore hips, to the cemetery. I walk through the vandalised gates, and the rank grass, among the graves. In my hand is a bunch of yellow flowers, picked from the cracks in the summer pavements, blended with a red tulip I found lying in the gutter.

I'm looking for my mother's grave. I know she is buried here. She was forty-three when she died. The crab ate her pomegranate womb.

But I can't find her, though I go up and down. There are always new headstones, and old ones that fall over, like the rest of us. Even graves are born, and die.

In the end, I leave my posy on the grave of a young girl, only seventeen – I work it out from her dates – when she died.

Perhaps she perished of a broken heart. So then, why not the rest of us?

Leaving the cemetery as the traffic of unwilling harsh morning gushes by, I feel I have been dutiful or merely tidy. Although I couldn't find my mother's tomb, I came to this place, where I know, or they have told me, it is. And so.

ABOUT THE AUTHOR

Tanith Lee (1947-2015) was born in London. Because her parents were professional dancers (ballroom, Latin American) and had to live where the work was, she attended a number of truly terrible schools, and didn't learn to read – she was also dyslectic – until almost age 8. And then only because her father taught her. This opened the world of books to her, and by 9 she was writing. After much better education at a grammar school, she went on to work in a library. This was followed by various other jobs – shop assistant, waitress, clerk – plus a year at art college when she was 25-26. In 1974, her career as a writer was launched, when DAW Books of America, under the leadership of Donald A. Wollheim, bought and published *The Birthgrave*, and thereafter 26 of her novels and collections.

Tanith was presented with a Lifetime Achievement Award in 2013, at World Fantasycon in Brighton. During her lifetime, she also received the World Horror Convention Grand Master Award, as well as the August Derleth Award and the World Fantasy Award for short fiction (twice).

In 1992, she married the writer-artist-photographer John Kaiine, her partner since 1987. They lived on the Sussex Weald, near the sea, in a house full of books and plants, and never without feline companions. She died at home in May 2015, after a long illness, continuing to work until a couple of weeks before her death.

Throughout her life, Tanith wrote around 100 books, and over 300 short stories. 4 of her radio plays were broadcast by the BBC; she also wrote 2 episodes (*Sarcophagus* and *Sand*) for the TV series *Blake's 7*. Her stories were read regularly on Radio 4 Extra. She was an inspiration to a generation of writers and her work was enormously influential within genre fiction – as it continues to be. She wrote in many styles, within and across many genres, including Horror, SF and Fantasy, Historical, Detective, Contemporary-Psychological, Children and Young Adult. Her preoccupation, though, was always people.

SELECTED BIBLIOGRAPHY OF TANITH LEE

The Birthgrave Trilogy (The Birthgrave; Vazkor, son of Vazkor, Quest for the White Witch)

The Vis Trilogy (The Storm Lord; Anackire; The White Serpent)

The Flat Earth Opus (Night's Master; Death's Master; Delusion's Master; Delirium's Mistress; Night's Sorceries)

Don't Bite the Sun

Drinking Sapphire Wine

Volkhavaar

The Paradys Quartet (The Book of the Damned; The Book of the Beast; The Book of the Dead; The Book of the Mad)

The Venus Quartet (Faces Under Water; Saint Fire; A Bed of Earth; Venus Preserved)

Kill the Dead

Electric Forest

Days of Grass

Sung in Shadow

A Heroine of the World

Sabella

Lycanthia

The Scarabae Blood Opera (Dark Dance; Personal Darkness; Darkness, I)

The Blood of Roses

When the Lights Go Out

Heart-Beast

Elephantasm

Eva Fairdeath

Reigning Cats and Dogs

Vivia

The Unicorn Trilogy (Black Unicorn; Gold Unicorn; Red Unicorn)

The Claidi Journals (Law of the Wolf Tower; Wolf Star Rise, Queen of the Wolves, Wolf Wing)

The Piratica Novels (Piratica 1; Piratica 2; Piratica 3)

The Silver Metal Lover

Metallic Love

Death of the Day

The Gods Are Thirsty

Mortal Suns

The Lionwolf Trilogy (Cast a Bright Shadow, Here in Cold Hell, No Flame But Mine)

COLLECTIONS
Nightshades
Dreams of Dark and Light
Forests of the Night
Women as Demons
Red as Blood – Tales from the Sisters Grimmer
Tamastara, or the Indian Nights
The Gorgon
Tempting the Gods
Hunting the Shadows
Sounds and Furies
Dancing in the Fire
Colder Greyer Stones
Space is Just a Starry Night
Phantasya
Blood 20

Also Published by Immanion Press
The Colouring Book Series
Greyglass
To Indigo
L'Amber
Killing Violets
Ivoria
Cruel Pink
Turquoiselle

Ghosteria Volume 1: The Stories
Ghosteria Volume 2: The Novel: Zircons May Be Mistaken
A Different City
Legenda Maris
Animate Objects
The Weird Tales of Tanith Lee

IMMANION PRESS

Purveyors of Speculative Fiction

The Lightbearer by Alan Richardson

Michael Horsett parachutes into Occupied France before the D-Day Invasion. He is dropped in the wrong place, miles from the action, badly injured, and totally alone. He falls prey to two Thelemist women who have awaited the Hawk God's coming, attracts a group of First World War veterans who rally to what they imagine is his cause, is hunted by a troop of German Field Police who are desperate to find him, and has a climactic encounter with a mutilated priest who believes that Lucifer Incarnate has arrived...

The Lightbearer is a unique gnostic thriller, dealing with the themes of Light and Darkness, Good and Evil, Matter and Spirit.

"The Lightbearer is another shining example of Alan Richardson's talent as a storyteller. He uses his wide esoteric knowledge to produce a story that thrills, chills and startles the reader as it radiates pure magical energy. An unusual and gripping war story with more facets than a star sapphire." – Mélusine Draco, author of "Aubry's Dog" and "Black Horse, White Horse". ISBN: 978-1-907737-63-3 £11.99 $18.99

Dark in the Day, Ed. by Storm Constantine & Paul Houghton

Weirdness lurks beyond the margins of the mundane, emerging to dismantle our assumptions of reality. Dark in the Day is an anthology of weird fiction, penned by established writers and also those new to the genre – the latter being authors who are, or were, students of Creative Writing at Staffordshire University, where editor Storm Constantine occasionally delivers guest lectures. Her co-editor, Paul Houghton, is the senior lecturer in Creative Writing at the university.

Contributors include: Martina Bellovičová, J. E. Bryant, Glynis Charlton, Storm Constantine, Louise Coquio, Elizabeth Counihan, Krishan Coupland, Elizabeth Davidson, Siân Davies, Paul Finch, Rosie Garland, Rhys Hughes, Kerry Fender, Andrew Hook, Paul Houghton, Tanith Lee, Tim Pratt, Nicholas Royle, Michael Marshall Smith, Paula Wakefield, Ian Whates and Liz Williams.
ISBN: 978-1-907737-74-9 £11.99, $18.99

Blood, the Phoenix and a Rose by Storm Constantine

Wraeththu, a race of androgynous beings, have arisen from the ashes of human civilisation. Like the mythical rebis, the divine hermaphrodite, they represent the pinnacle of human evolution. But Wraeththu – or hara – were forged in the crucible of destruction and emerged from a new Dark Age. They have yet to realise their full potential and come to terms with the most blighted aspects of their past. Blood, the Phoenix and a Rose begins with an enigma: Gavensel, a har who appears unearthly and has a shrouded history. He has been hidden away in the house of Sallow Gandaloi by Melisander, an alchemist, but is this seclusion to protect Gavensel from the world or the world from him? As his story unfolds, the shadow of the dark fortress Fulminir falls over him, and memories of his past slowly return. The only way to find the truth is to go back through the layers of time, to when the blood was fresh. ISBN: 978-1-907737-75-6 £11.99, $18.99

The Weird Tales of Tanith Lee

"A story by Tanith Lee unveils a voice alone, a true Scheherazade, someone with a distinctive vision of the world and who explored that world, or those worlds to be accurate, with a highly perceptive and mindful set of eyes."

From the introduction, by Mike Ashley

This anthology of twenty-eight tales comprises all the short stories by Tanith Lee that were published in the seminal magazine *Weird Tales* during her lifetime. Some of them are previously uncollected, and appeared in print only in the magazine, so will be new to many of Tanith's fans. Her highly-respected and influential work spanned every genre, and this sumptuous collection demonstrates the range of her versatility. From the dark high fantasy of 'The Sombrus Tower', through the Arthurian-influenced 'The Kingdoms of the Air', the achingly beautiful 'Stars Above, Stars Below' of a science-fantasy Mars, the sinister retelling of a fairy tale in 'When the Clock Strikes', and the almost whimsical steampunk of 'The Persecution Machine', *The Weird Tales of Tanith Lee* showcases the myriad styles of the writer rightly known as the High Priestess of Fantasy.

ISBN: 978-1-907737-73-2, £11.99 $18.99

Immanion Press
http://www.immanion-press.com
info@immanion-press.com

Fatal Women: The Esther Garber Novellas, by Tanith Lee
ISBN: 9781590213100 $16.00, pbk, 330 pages
Tanith Lee channels the elusive Esther Garber to tell these dark, erotic tales of lesbian ardor and obsession. The "fatal women" found within these pages lead exotic lives and adventures and have grim secrets. From *fin de siècle* Paris to Egypt of the 1930s and contemporary England, the Garber novellas create feverish dreams of danger, scandal, and sensuality. This new edition includes the novella "Femme Fatale," never before in print, as well as an essay by Mavis Haut, author of *The Hidden Library of Tanith Lee*, about the eminence of this collection within Lee's body of work.

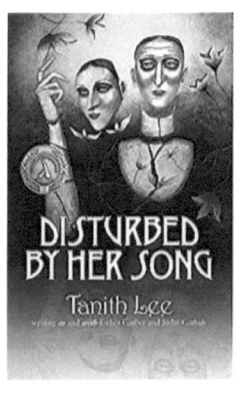

Disturbed by Her Song, by Tanith Lee
ISBN: 9781590213117, $16.00, pbk, 204 pages
Disturbed By Her Song collects the work of Esther Garber and her half-brother Judas Garbah, the mysterious family of writers that Tanith Lee has been channeling for the past few years. Possibly autobiographical, frequently erotic and darkly surreal, their fiction takes place in a variety of eras and places, from Egypt in the 1940s, to England in the grip of the Pre-Raphaelites, to gaslit Paris and to the shadowy landscapes carved by the mind and memory. The themes of youth and age stream through these tales of homosexual love and desire. These stories recall, at times, the work of Lawrence Durrell, Colette, and Angela Carter.

http://www.lethepressbooks.com/

NEWCON PRESS

http://newconpress.co.uk/

The very best in fantasy, science fiction, and horror

Colder Greyer Stones by **Tanith Lee**

Released to commemorate the author being honoured with a Lifetime Achievement Award at the 2013 World Fantasy Convention, this stunning collection of stories provides further evidence of why Tanith Lee is held in such high regard by fans and contemporaries alike. The book features twelve wonderful, rich-textured tales, including the brand-new novelette "The Frost Watcher" and five stories previously available only in the (sold out) signed limited edition "Cold Grey Stones".

Paperback: ISBN 978-1-907069-60-4 £9.99

Visionary Tongue edited by **Storm Constantine**

"The visionary tongue speaks. Now listen to its voice." – Storm Constantine

Founder and original editor Storm Constantine has revisited every issue of the ground-breaking magazine *Visionary Tongue* to select the very best stories and poems to appear in its pages across a twelve-year period, more than thirty in all, including early stories from some of the UK genre scene's biggest names, including Liz Williams, Tim Lebbon, Justina Robson and Jaine Fenn.

Available as an A5 paperback and a numbered limited-edition hardback signed by the editor. The limited edition includes four bonus stories not available elsewhere.

ISBN: 978-1-910935-60-6 pbk £12.99 ISBN: 978-1-910935-59-0 hbk £24.99

www.ingramcontent.com/pod-product-compliance
Lightning Source LLC
Chambersburg PA
CBHW020914180626
46816CB00007BA/2398